The Love Beat Goes On

by

Cynthia Breeding

Nostalgia Road: The Sixties

Cover Art by *The Wild Rose Press, Inc.*

The Wild Rose Press, Inc.
PO Box 708
Adams Basin, NY 14410-0708
Visit us at www.thewildrosepress.com

Publishing History
First Edition, 2025
Trade Paperback ISBN 978-1-5092-6265-6
Digital ISBN 978-1-5092-6266-3

Nostalgia Road: The Sixties
Previously Published Highland Press 2018
Published in the United States of America

Chapter One

December, 1967

"That was, like, the best movie, *ever*," Wendy Wade looked at her cousin Jo as the credits rolled for *Camelot*. "I'm definitely going to find my very own knight in shining armor in 1968."

"I'm not sure if the movie made me feel glad or sad," Jo answered as they walked out of the theatre into the bracing cold air of a Minnesota afternoon. "I know I could never cheat on Luke, even if we weren't going steady."

Wendy refrained from rolling her eyes. Even though Luke was away at college in St. Cloud, Jo got a letter every day and she probably wrote him two. If long distance calling weren't so expensive, they'd be on the phone for hours. "I didn't mean the cheating part. I meant the knights having courage, being honorable, and acting courtly to please their ladies. The whole concept of the Round Table is about everyone being equal and respecting each other. And only fighting for just causes. Not like the Vietnam thing."

Jo raised an eyebrow. "I suppose that depends on whom you'd ask. Some people think we're doing the right thing by defending the South Vietnamese from Communism."

"Like who? There are anti-war protests going on

everywhere, except maybe here in Middletown." Wendy grinned. "Can you imagine our teachers if we all showed up at school carrying signs and wearing flowers in our hair?"

"Where would we find flowers this time of year?"

Wendy loved her cousin, but Jo took things too literally sometimes. "I meant, wouldn't it be fun to shock our teachers just once before we graduate in the spring? We are *so* Mayberry RFD here."

"I like it," Jo said. "When I lived in Brooklyn, everything was hustle and bustle. Not to mention high rates of crime. Your knights would have had their hands full fighting that."

"They'd have handled it," Wendy replied. "I can almost see all of them charging down the street on white horses, brandishing swords and making the criminals run away."

Jo shook her head. "You haven't been on a Brooklyn street. The good guys don't always win."

"But they should." Wendy sobered. "You're right though. We sure aren't winning in Vietnam."

"I don't know," Jo said. "President Johnson just reaffirmed this fall that progress is being made."

"Big deal," Wendy replied. "Governor Reagan in California says we should get out of Vietnam too."

Jo gave her a teasing look. "What else would you expect from the leader of a state that just hosted the great Summer of Love?"

"Hmph. The flower-power thing is pretty much over," Wendy answered, "although probably a lot of the hippies still drifting around San Francisco have draft cards waiting at home."

Jo shrugged. "Which they'd probably just burn."

"That isn't right either." Wendy frowned. "That's as bad as the draft dodgers running off to Canada."

"True," Jo said as they reached their car, "but I guess it's their way of protesting."

"It's not the same," Wendy answered as she opened her door. "I mean, King Arthur's knights adhered to their Code of Chivalry even when they disagreed. Why can't Americans obey our laws too?"

"I don't have the answer." Jo smiled at her. "But Camelot really only exists in our dreams."

...only in our dreams. Wendy frowned again. She didn't want to believe that. Somewhere a knight—maybe not wearing shining armor—waited for her. She knew he did.

****

Snow had begun falling when Wendy and Jo stepped outside school Friday afternoon before the holidays.

"It looks like we'll have a white Christmas!" Wendy turned her face skyward and stuck out her tongue to catch a snowflake. Although it had been cold, there'd only been flurries that didn't stick. "Maybe we can get the horse sleigh out for caroling."

"That's a week away," a male voice said from behind her. "Our escape from prison will be half over!"

Wendy turned to see Tim and Tommy, her twin cousins, clambering down the steps to join them. Both of them wore mischievous grins and she wondered if they'd managed to pull some pre-holiday prank, which was highly likely. She gave each of them a suspicious glance. "Have you been up to something?"

Tommy widened his eyes innocently while Tim managed a hurt look before he spoke. "Why would you

3

say that?"

She wasn't fooled by either of their expressions or by Tim's benign tone. The more innocent they sounded, the more guilty they usually were. "What did you do?"

"Nothing…" Tommy widened his grin. "…much."

"Really. It was just a *little* thing," Tim said and slapped his brother on the back which caused them both to howl.

Wendy narrowed her eyes. "Don't tell me you put spiders in Mrs. Howell's desk again. She fainted last year when she opened the drawer."

"We've grown up since then." Tim's voice was full of righteous indignation. "We're seniors now."

"Besides, we decided we like the English teacher, even if she thinks Shakespeare is great," Tommy added.

"Shakespeare *is* great," Jo said. "You just need to appreciate the language."

Momentarily, the twins stared at her as though she'd taken leave of her senses. Then Tim shrugged. "You make straight A's, don't you?"

"A goal that wouldn't hurt you to try for," Wendy said before Jo could answer. "You guys need to get into college."

"More prison time," Tommy said.

"Maybe she has a point," Tim said. "There are girls there."

Wendy shook her head. Trying to get the twins to be serious was a losing battle. "So what exactly have you done this time? Left the water running in the boys' room to flood the halls?"

Tommy assumed the indignant look this time. "Of course not. We did that in middle school."

"We've *matured*."

"That must have been fast," Wendy retorted. "Just after Thanksgiving, you put turkey feathers in Mrs. Todd's office wastebasket where the electrical fan she always uses would blow them everywhere."

Tim chortled. "You have to admit The Hound looked pretty funny with feathers stuck to him."

Wendy grimaced. "The Hound" referred to the vice-principal, whose name, Hund, meant "dog" in German. That he looked rather like a bulldog with his heavy jowls and perpetual glowering face, didn't help matters. He'd also been a former coach and could bark commands heard clearly down any hall.

"That little stunt got you both a week of detention," Jo said.

"The Hound has no sense of humor," Tommy said.

Tim nodded. "He should have listened to the secretary. She wasn't mad."

"Only because you guys flirt with her every time you get sent to the office," Jo answered.

"We can't help it if we're likable," Tim said.

Tommy grinned. "And good-looking."

Wendy shook her head again. The twins *were* good-looking. They resembled the current heart throb everyone was calling 'Troy" with their dark-blond hair and green eyes. Their looks, along with their ability to apologize profusely in what sounded like the most sincere tones, usually kept them from too dire consequences. Usually. But Mr. Hund wasn't that easily fooled.

"So what did you *do*?"

Tim shrugged. "We aren't saying."

"We wouldn't want you to become accomplices." Tommy grinned. "You should thank us for looking out for you."

Jo looked heavenward. "How chivalrous."

"Our pleasure, ladies. Just call us Sir Knights," Tim said as both the twins bowed and then sauntered away, still grinning.

Wendy watched them leave and gave a very unladylike snort. Unfortunately, they'd seen *Camelot* too.

"Not exactly your idea of chivalrous knights?" Jo asked teasingly.

"Hardly." Wendy started walking toward the school bus waiting to take the country kids home. "They're nincompoops."

"Who will hopefully make it to graduation without getting expelled," Jo said as she followed.

Wendy glanced at her. When Jo had come to live with them after her parents were killed in a car accident two years ago, she'd not liked the twins. Not that Wendy could blame her. The pranks they'd pulled to embarrass her in front of Luke weren't funny. Given that everything had worked out between her and Luke anyway, Jo had gradually forgiven them. Wendy was pretty sure that was a testimony to Jo's character rather than the twins' ability to get themselves out of trouble.

She snorted. Chivalrous knights indeed.

****

"You got your wish for a white Christmas," Jo told Wendy as they both sat in front of the living room window staring at white-out conditions for the fourth day in a row. "I'm sure Tim and Tommy are grumbling that this should have happened while school was still in session."

"We would have had to make the days up over

Easter break," Wendy answered. "They'd have grumbled about that too."

Not that she wasn't tired of being housebound. A good three feet of snow blanketed the landscape, and drifts from the howling wind had accumulated to six and seven feet in places, even reaching to the eaves of the farmhouse. They'd tied a rope to the porch railing and trailed it across the yard to the barn, tying the other end to the hitching rail, so they could follow the tether out to feed the horses and back to the house and not get disoriented in the blinding snow.

"I guess I should be careful what I wish for," she said.

"You can't blame yourself for the weather," Jo replied.

"I'm not so sure. I *prayed* for snow."

Jo smiled. "Then pray that it stops."

She'd done that too. They'd already missed the annual Yuletide wassail-caroling that was held in the town square every December 21st, and last minute shopping trips had been curtailed. Worst though, the blizzard conditions prevented the snowplows from keeping the roads open, which meant Wendy's sister, Mary Anne, and her boyfriend James were stuck in Minneapolis. Luke couldn't get home from St. Cloud, either.

"You haven't seen Luke for a month," Wendy said. "You must be about ready to scream."

"If that would help, I'd do it. But I'd rather have him be safe than take a risk on the roads." Jo sighed and squinted at the swirling snow. "I guess we can celebrate Christmas after the actual day, if we have to."

Wendy didn't even want to think how disappointed

her mother would be if Mary Anne, James, and Luke didn't make it home for Christmas. It was always a big thing at their house. After attending church and opening their gifts on Christmas morning, they would have a huge buffet later that included roast beef, ham, and turkey along with various casseroles, yams, mashed potatoes and gravy, yeast rolls and a dozen pies as well. Neighbors would drift in and out all afternoon. The day would be chaotic and noisy, but in the evening, when the neighbors had gone home, the family would gather around the Christmas tree for three verses of *Silent Night* before the lights were turned out and peace fell, if not on earth, at least on the household.

She said another silent prayer that the weather would improve.

****

Her prayer was answered. Christmas Eve day dawned bright and clear, although bitterly cold. Not that anyone noticed, since the kitchen oven and stove were going the entire day getting the food ready for the Christmas buffet. By midafternoon, Luke arrived, much to Jo's delight, although they had little time for privacy since he was put to work in the kitchen. James dropped Mary Anne off later and, to Wendy's surprise, her somewhat jaded sister tossed off an expensive sweater and pitched in to help. James must have had a really positive effect on her, but there was no time for questions since her mother was giving orders with the efficiency of a five-star general.

By the time all the food had been prepared and put into the extra refrigerators in the garage, Wendy was ready to drop. James had arrived earlier to whisk Mary Anne off to his family's Christmas Eve celebration. Luke had taken Jo over to his father's for the evening, along with her mother since the two widowed parents had developed a friendship over the past year.

Wendy had been invited to go, but she'd declined, not wanting to be a fifth wheel, even if it was her family. Now she wondered if she'd made a mistake. The farmhouse was big and rambling, but it was eerily quiet. No prancing reindeer on the roof. No horses stamping their hooves outside either. They were all tucked into warm stalls, probably munching on sweet hay.

Tonight the house seemed…lonely. The silence was so total that Wendy strained her ears for any sounds from outside and then shook her head as she started up the stairs to her room. What had she been expecting? Sir Galahad to ride up to the door?

She paused, listening to the faint ticking of a grandfather clock at the end of the hall. Time was passing. Maybe by next Christmas she would have found her knight.

****

"There isn't room for everyone in the sleigh," Wendy said the afternoon after Christmas. "You guys go ahead."

"There's room if we all crunch together." Tommy put an arm around his girlfriend Susan and pulled her closer.

"Good idea." Tim grinned and tugged his own girlfriend Carla onto his lap, causing her to giggle. "This will keep us warmer anyhow."

"Really, guys. It's crowded."

"Please get in." Jo turned on the driver's bench she was sharing with Luke and looked down. "You need to have some fun since you didn't go with us on Christmas

Eve and yesterday you kept busy in the kitchen."

There was a reason for that, but Wendy didn't say anything as she climbed into the sleigh beside Mary Anne and James. Everyone was couples except for herself. She was happy for all of them, she was, but she also felt that she stuck out like a sore thumb.

The twins' girlfriends were nestled against them, already cooing and probably would be making out the minute they were away from prying adult eyes. Jo had her hand looped through Luke's arm where she could look at the tiny diamond winking on her finger. It was called a "promise ring" and meant they were practically engaged. She and Luke had shown it off after all the neighbors had gone last night. And now, although Luke was in charge of driving the sleigh, he managed to look at Jo every few seconds and give her a smile, which Jo returned. She deserved her happiness.

Wendy was happy for her sister, too. Last year, Mary Anne had run away to San Francisco after Bob, the guy she'd been in love with, dumped her for a pregnant girlfriend. Her sister had thought the hippie lifestyle would give her freedom, only she'd been robbed and, with no money and no job, couldn't get home. James had flown out and found her at the Panhandle of Golden Gate Park where there was free food. They'd become a couple once they returned, and now Mary Anne was wearing a buttery soft leather jacket that James had gotten her for Christmas and kept saying how beautiful and warm it was.

It had been a wonderful Christmas for all of them, and Wendy had managed to keep a smile plastered on her face until it was beginning to ache. Maybe, with as cold as the temperature was, the sleigh ride wouldn't be long. Things would be better once everyone was back in school.

They'd not gone too far when James leaned across Mary Anne and smiled at Wendy. "I almost forgot. My mother said she'd gotten a letter from the Foreign Exchange Student Program last week. Do you remember Kevin O'Keefe, the guy we hosted who had to leave and go back to Ireland?"

"Sure. Why?"

"It looks like he'll be returning." James winked. "You'd better get ready."

Wendy felt her cheeks warm although whether from embarrassment, anticipation, or indignation, she wasn't sure. His declaration had managed to ignite all three.

She certainly hadn't expected to see Kevin O'Keefe again.

Chapter Two

The twins stopped smooching their girlfriends at James' remark and Mary Anne looked at Wendy curiously.

"Kevin had a thing for you, didn't he?"

Wendy's face grew warmer and she hoped everyone would think the redness of her cheeks was from the cold. Last year, everyone had said Kevin liked her, but she had been too gaga over James to notice. James, of course, only had eyes for Mary Anne, a small fact Wendy had ignored, although Kevin hadn't. In the letter he'd left her when he returned to Ireland, he had quite bluntly pointed out she was wasting her time yearning for James and hoped she'd be happy for her sister.

She'd never shown the letter to anyone, but she still smarted from it. Kevin was right, but that only made matters worse since she'd obviously been too blind to notice. And she didn't like the fact that he'd practically given her *advice* on how to be mature when he was the same age, for Pete's sake.

"Kevin was nice to everyone," she said neutrally.

"Yeah, but he always managed to sit at your lunch table," Tim said.

Tommy grinned. "And give you his dessert."

"Not that often!" Wendy shot back. "It was probably when he didn't like something."

"Or something *you* really did," Tommy answered,

not to be deterred when he found someone to tease. "Let's see, you like cookies and cake and pie—"

"Who doesn't?" Wendy glared at him, hoping none of them would recall all the times she had eaten Kevin's desserts. "And you're going to make me hungry talking about food."

"Trying to change the subject?" Tim asked, unwilling to be outdone by his twin when it came to badgering someone. "Okay. Let's see. I think I remember a special assignment you guys worked on together—"

"That was *my* assignment," Mary Anne cut in. "Ruby and I had been talking in English class and got that as punishment. James helped bail us out."

"Ah, yes." Tommy assumed a thoughtful expression, which meant he was up to something. "And Wendy was with you in the library after school because…?"

Dear Lord. Could her face get any hotter? Wendy felt as though she was about to spontaneously combust. Like a moonstruck calf, she had tagged along on that project so she could be near James. She didn't need to be reminded how stupid she'd been, especially with James sitting right there.

James gave Tommy an even look. "If I remember correctly, Mary Anne had the family car and Wendy needed rides home."

Bless James for saving her from total embarrassment. But then, he'd always been kind. Mary Anne had really lucked out on finding *her* knight.

"Well, there was always the school bus…" Tim's voice trailed off when James turned his steady gaze on him and he swallowed. "…I guess the car would have been better, though."

"Of course it was." Jo looked over her shoulder at them. "And don't forget that Kevin was staying at James' house, so he needed a ride home too."

"Whatever," Tim replied, apparently finally realizing it was time to stop the goading. "That was last year anyhow."

"Yeah," Tommy added. "Besides, our other foreign exchange student, Bridget McBride, is from Ireland too. Maybe they'll hit it off together."

Wendy felt a twinge of something that felt a little like jealousy. Bridget had arrived in September and was in her English and government classes. She had inky hair that curled around her shoulders, blue eyes that were nearly violet, and a creamy-smooth complexion. Some of the boys said she looked like Elizabeth Taylor.

"Maybe it takes the luck of the Irish with her." Tim shrugged. "I heard some of the guys say she turned them down for dates."

"Probably just stuck-up," Tommy said.

"I don't think she's stuck-up at all. She's always been nice when Wendy and I have talked to her," Jo replied and looked at Wendy. "Hasn't she?"

Wendy nodded. She couldn't fault Bridget for that. If anything, she seemed a bit shy, not that they had had any long talks or anything.

The twins' girlfriends evidently were tired of talk about another girl since they both started cuddling again with Tim and Tommy. Mary Anne laid her head against James' shoulder and Jo turned back around to talk to Luke. For long minutes, all that could be heard was the tinkling of the bells attached to the horse's harness and the steady slide of the sled's blades through the snow.

Wendy was grateful the battering of questions concerning Kevin had stopped, but now the thought that he probably would hit it off with a pretty girl from his own country kept niggling at her. Not that she should care. He had written her that bossy-sounding letter, after all. And he hadn't said anything about her being special, either, in that dumb letter. Had she been? She hadn't paid much attention last year, silly as her unrequited feelings for James had been. What would Kevin be like this year?

And, more importantly, with whom would he be having lunch?

****

She needn't have worried about lunch their first day back in January. Kevin wasn't in attendance. As she and Jo sat at a table unwrapping chicken salad sandwiches, she searched the lunchroom once more.

"I don't think you're going to conjure him up." Jo opened a bag of chips and dumped half on Wendy's tray. "Kevin isn't here."

"But James said he would be." Wendy knew she sounded plaintive and cleared her throat. "Maybe the exchange program sent him somewhere else."

Jo shook her head. "The Lambarts hosted him last year and they requested him back if he returned. They wouldn't have received a letter confirming that if he was being sent somewhere else."

"It seems strange that he'd miss the first day of the semester, though."

"James did say Kevin wouldn't get here until this weekend. His flight might have been delayed since that blizzard we had moved into the northeast. Or maybe he's in the other lunch shift." Jo gave her a quizzical look. "I thought you weren't all that interested in Kevin."

Wendy shrugged, hoping she looked nonchalant. "It's not like I'm *interested* interested. It's just…well…"

"It's okay. You don't have to admit anything." Jo smiled. "He was awfully cute, though."

"I didn't think you even noticed any guy except Luke."

Her smile widened. "No one can top Luke, but I'd have to be totally blind not to notice. Don't tell me you don't think Kevin's cute."

Wendy took a bite of her sandwich, chewing slowly so she wouldn't have to answer right away. Last year when she'd been infatuated with James, she hadn't paid much attention to Kevin, although now she realized he really had been…*striking*, more so than cute. He had dark auburn hair long enough to touch his collar, which somehow had escaped The Hound's attention, but it was his eyes that really were compelling. They had an unusual golden tone—whiskey-colored, her mother had said—that brought out the burnished strands in the stubborn lock of hair that continually fell over his forehead.

"Sure. He's okay."

"Right." Jo started to roll her eyes and then stopped suddenly to stare over Wendy's shoulder.

"What?"

"Kevin's here. He just walked in."

Wendy told herself not to jerk around to look. Somehow she managed a slow turn to look at the cafeteria door, but she couldn't stop her sharp inhalation at the sight of him standing beside Mrs. Jones, the school counselor.

In the year he'd been gone, he seemed to have grown. He was taller by a couple of inches. He'd added muscle, too, and his shoulders were definitely broader. Even from halfway across the cafeteria she could see how much more mature he looked. His hair was still longish, but the planes of his face—the high cheekbones, straight nose, and firm jaw —had somehow become more chiseled-looking. Probably the shock of his father's death last year and having to make sure his family was okay had done that. In any case, he looked more like a man than a boy.

"You're staring." Jo nudged her. "What do you think?"

Wendy forced her gaze away from him. "He looks…more grown up."

"Losing your parents—even one of them—can do that," Jo said.

Wendy squeezed her hand. She'd lost her father when she was seven, but Jo had lost both parents only three years ago. "I guess we all have something in common then."

Jo nodded. "It takes time to…oh, oh."

"What?" Wendy wanted to turn around, but she didn't want to be caught staring. "Is Kevin coming this way?"

"Ah… no." Jo frowned slightly. "Mrs. Jones is—"

"What?" Wendy gave in to her desire to turn around and then felt as though her horse Jupiter had suddenly kicked her in the stomach.

Mrs. Jones was introducing Kevin to Bridget. He grinned—Wendy had forgotten how beguiling that smile was. Bridget smiled back and then gestured toward a table. Kevin nodded and they moved away together.

Her invisible horse's other hoof struck Wendy. She put her sandwich down, unable to eat another bite.

****

As Wendy took her seat in last period Government class, she wondered if Kevin had a totally different schedule from hers. She didn't know about the morning classes since he'd been registering with the counselor, but she hadn't seen him in her two afternoon classes. She and Jo had different schedules after lunch as well, so she hadn't been able to talk to her.

Glancing over at Bridget, who sat near the door, the thought occurred that maybe Kevin had been in classes with the Irish girl since lunch. The idea was disturbing and Wendy pushed it away. Bridget was a nice person and it was only logical that Mrs. Jones would have introduced Kevin to a fellow exchange student from the same country. It was also totally *illogical* to be jealous. It wasn't like she and Kevin had actually dated.

Kevin had a thing for you, didn't he?

Wendy recalled Mary Anne's words during the sleigh ride. Jo had said practically the same thing later when they'd had a chance to talk, pointing out that Kevin hung around after school to help with Mary Anne and James' project because *she* hung around to do the same. And, she knew the reason she did—she'd been besotted with James. Had Kevin been besotted with her?

He *had* always offered her his desserts… She sighed. Here she was, telling Jo she wanted to find a knight in shining armor and Kevin—minus the outfit— had really fit the bill. She'd just been too silly to see it. Did she dare hope he still liked her…really *liked* her? Would he be willing to be her knight now?

"Someone looks lovelorn." Tim slipped into the empty seat beside her and grinned. "Anyone special?"

"Like maybe Kevin?" Tommy snickered and took

the seat behind her.

Wendy groaned inwardly. She was going to have to be careful if she didn't want the twins teasing her unmercifully—or worse, telling Kevin she was pining for him. Not that she was. She wasn't. Still…

"Don't be silly. I haven't even talked to him."

"That's because he was in Woodshop and Agriculture with us," Tim said.

She breathed a sigh of relief. No classes with Bridget then, since neither the woodshop nor the ag teachers allowed girls. But not having girls around would give her cousins ample opportunity to fill Kevin's head with whatever inclinations they thought would be funny. Everyone knew the twins had a warped sense of humor, so better to play like she had no interest.

"I just hope tragedy doesn't strike again."

"Tragedy?" Tommy formed his hand around an invisible microphone and began sotto-voce, "*Oh, come back, have me here…*"

Tim followed suit. "*Hold me love, be sincere…*"

"*Whoa-whoa, TRAGEDY.*" Both twins sang the finish to the Fleetwoods' song.

"Shhh!" Wendy hissed. "Will you shut up?"

"Well, geez." Tommy blinked. "Don't freak out."

"Yeah, we could do another song if you don't like that one," Tim said. "How about—"

"*Shut up*," Wendy whispered furiously as Mr. Kyle came into the room. "You're not funny."

Evidently, she'd spoken the last part too loudly, for the teacher raised an eyebrow. "I wasn't aware I needed to be a comedian."

The twins sniggled.

Mr. Kyle directed a look at them. "Then again, given

the state of politics these days, perhaps some levity in a government class is needed." He turned back to Wendy. "Would you agree, Miss Wade?"

"I…" To her mortification, Kevin walked in at that moment. His gaze, as if by magnetic contact, connected to hers. She stared at him, sure her face was as red as the sweater she'd worn. Tim gave her a knowing look while, behind her, Tommy snickered again. She narrowed her eyes. She was going to *throttle* her cousins. She looked quickly away before she could give them any food for thought and busied herself taking out a notebook.

Mr. Kyle turned his attention to Kevin. "You must be our new foreign exchange student. Mrs. Jones said to be expecting you."

"Aye, sir." Kevin handed him a paper. "She said ye would be needin' this."

The light lilt to his brogue washed over Wendy like warm waves on a summer lake. She'd forgotten his soft accent. She wanted desperately to look up, but her blasted cousins were watching her like hawks ready to pounce. She flipped a page in her binder, pretending to study her notes.

"Ah, yes. Your enrollment form. Very good." Mr. Kyle gestured. "Perhaps you'd like to have a seat next to Bridget, our other foreign exchange student? She's from Ireland too."

"Aye, we met a lunch," Kevin answered and then smiled at Bridget as he took the seat next to her. "'Tis good to see ye again, lass."

Bridget gave him a big smile back. "And 'tis pleased I am to be hearin' a familiar voice."

Wendy concentrated on her notes for real, having no desire any longer to look up. And she didn't need to hear any more talk, either.

From anyone.

****

Kevin settled into the chair hoping he looked calmer than he felt. Even though there had been a six-hour delay at LaGuardia causing him to miss his connection to Minneapolis on Saturday, so he'd gotten to Middletown late yesterday dead-tired, he'd awakened this morning with renewed energy. Today, he'd finally be seeing Wendy again.

It had been all he could think about on the long flight over. He'd been attracted to her from the first time he saw her in English class last year. She'd been wearing a simple blue shirt that matched her eyes, denim jeans and cowboy boots that looked well worn. He remembered James teasing him that it was the boots that hooked him since Kevin's father had trained Thoroughbreds and he'd grown up with horses, but the boots only proved they had something in common. He'd been intrigued with the sprinkling of freckles across her nose. She wore no makeup, but instead of looking plain, she looked refreshing, like an Irish glade in the morning after the mist had lifted. He'd also been fascinated with the way her ponytail bounced when she walked. Her personality was bouncy too...open and friendly and curious. She reminded him a little of Sandra Dee from the *Gidget* movies, except Wendy's hair was brown, not blonde.

And now here he was, finally back in class with her again.

Only she hadn't acknowledged him. He'd spotted her immediately, only she had narrowed her eyes and then looked quickly away. Why?

Kevin looked casually over his shoulder. Wendy

was still engrossed in whatever was written in her notebook. Something from a boyfriend, maybe? He frowned. James hadn't mentioned that she was seeing anyone, but then, he'd been at the University of Minnesota for the past semester.

Since her twin cousins were watching him, one with a little smirk and the other with a more appraising expression, Kevin turned around. Until he found out how things stood around here, it would be better to appear neutral. He wasn't about to act like a love-starved puppy again.

As Mr. Kyle began passing back worksheets, Bridget leaned over to whisper. "I ken this sounds silly, but 'tis so good to hear an Irish accent again. I've been missin' my home."

Kevin smiled at her. He remembered he'd been a little homesick when he'd first arrived in the States last year as well, although that had quickly passed once he'd seen Wendy. Bridget had told him at lunch the family hosting her had lost their only son to a football injury last year and wanted a young person in the house, but it meant she didn't have a foster sister or brother like he'd had, so she was probably lonely. She also looked a lot like his sister Mary, who'd spent weeks crying after their father's death.

"Doona fash over it." Kevin patted Bridget's hand briefly. "You've got a friend from home now."

Chapter Three

"Don't look so glum. You'll get a chance to talk to Kevin tomorrow," Jo told Wendy as they got on the school bus to go home. "Or you could call him tonight."

"He'll think I'm chasing him," Wendy answered. "Boys are supposed to do the calling."

"That old rule is kind of changing. Girls don't need to wait anymore," Jo said. "Besides, you can just say 'welcome back' since he had to leave class before the bell today."

Wendy frowned. Just before Mr. Kyle had gotten a note from the office that Kevin needed to fill out more paperwork, she'd decided she'd bump into Kevin at the door as they left, making sure it looked accidental, so neither of the twins got suspicious. But then, the teacher had dismissed him early to go to the office. As he'd turned to leave, Bridget waved at him and he'd nodded to her, not looking back at the rest of the class.

"I don't know. You remember how Mom got upset when Mary Anne ran after Bob last year."

"That was different. Bob was older and smoked cigarettes, not to mention getting Mary Anne drunk one time. Aunt Viv *likes* Kevin," Jo replied.

"Still. The boy should call." Wendy'd noticed the whispering Kevin had done with Bridget, and also seen him touch her hand. Bridget had given him a big smile. And they'd had lunch together, although that was because of the counselor. But Kevin hadn't sought *her* out, so she felt really stupid about calling him. "At least, the boy should make the first call."

Jo rolled her eyes. "This is Kevin, remember? The guy who hung around you all the time."

She winced. She'd blown that. And this Kevin seemed different from last year's Kevin. He'd gone from cute to handsome, but he seemed more serious and not the happy-go-lucky boy he'd been. *That* boy had teased her and followed her around. She sensed this Kevin might not be so willing to do that. But she wouldn't know until she could *talk* to him.

"He wasn't exactly hanging around me today."

"Cut him some slack. He just got here." Jo gave her a quick glance. "I don't think you need to be jealous of Bridget."

Wendy sometimes wondered if Jo had the ability to read minds. "I didn't say I was."

Her cousin smiled. "I saw your expression at lunch."

"That isn't the half of it," Wendy answered before she could stop herself.

"What do you mean?"

"Never mind."

"Uh-uh. You know I won't leave you alone until you tell me."

"You're as bad as the twins," Wendy grumbled.

"Pul—eeze! Their motives for being nosy are entirely different."

"Well, that's true, I guess." Wendy proceeded to tell her what had transpired in government class. "I don't know if I can compete with Bridget."

"Remember when I thought I was competing with Amy for Luke?" Jo asked. "That caused me a lot of sleepless nights and turned out to be nothing."

"But Luke and Amy weren't from the same foreign country."

"No, but they had a lot in common and Amy was really smart and nice."

"So is Bridget." Wendy grimaced. "That doesn't exactly help."

"Your mom always says it's no use to create problems before they occur," Jo said. "So don't worry. Things will work out."

Wendy reluctantly nodded, not wanting to prolong the discussion. It was easy for her cousin to say that since she and Luke were already thinking about getting married someday. But Wendy wasn't even sure Kevin liked her anymore, like he had before. And she couldn't run after him. It would be too humiliating if he ignored her. She'd die of embarrassment if he did. She would.

****

Wendy approached government class the next day with mixed emotions. It had been disappointing to find out Kevin was not in any of her morning classes, but he had made his way over to her and Jo at lunch. Unfortunately, the twins were already at the table as well, so conversation had been limited to what had taken place while he was gone. The bright point had been to learn that he'd be using James' horse to join their saddle club on their Saturday morning rides. The down side was that probably wouldn't happen for at least a couple of months, not until the weather got warmer and most of the snow melted, but it would definitely give Wendy a chance to get to know him again away from school. She just hoped Bridget didn't ride.

"All right, class," Mr. Kyle said as the bell rang. "I

need to explain the project we'll be doing to launch 1968. A new year. And hopefully, a better one."

Half of the class nodded, since 1967 had been so tumultuous. The news had been full of young people revolting, some of them staging sit-ins for peace and others running off to San Francisco to join communes, do drugs, and rebel against the Establishment. Still more protested the war-that-wasn't-a-war in Vietnam. Fifty thousand had marched in Washington, to no avail. Guys not in college left for Canada to avoid the draft. Riots had sprung up in Detroit and across the nation as the Civil Rights Movement carried on.

Wendy agreed with Mr. Kyle. 1968 had to be better.

"This cultural and social project is going to last most of the spring semester," Mr. Kyle said, "and will be composed of three parts: the on-going conflict in Vietnam, progress in the Civil Rights movement, and how to combat drug abuse." A few students snickered at that and he gave them a stern look. "Although I expect to hear lots of debate on the Vietnam issue as well as the best ways to implement Civil Rights, the *only* thing we will be discussing concerning drugs is how to curtail their use."

"So we can't talk about hippies?" Tommy asked. "They're the ones using the stuff."

"And what about communes?" Tim added. "They're cultural."

The teacher gave both of them a resigned look. "Actually, they are counter-cultural, but yes, that will obviously be part of your research. Now, I'm going to divide you into groups of four. You will be a part of a team and I expect each one of you to carry your full load."

Wendy smirked when Mr. Kyle assigned the twins to different groups. He apparently wasn't going to allow them to join forces to argue with him. Then her small smile faded as the teacher put Lionel Jackson into Tommy's group.

Lionel was a new student this year. And he was the first black student at Middletown and probably for twenty miles around, too. His father had taken a job as assistant foreman at the manufacturing plant down the road and his family had moved from Detroit over the summer.

Besides Lionel, there were four other kids in his family. LaShonda was a junior, Lysander attended middle school, and Leah and Leonard were in elementary. She had thought it cute that all their names started with an L. They had the same last name of that new musical group, the Jackson brothers, except of course, LaShonda and Leah were girls. She just hoped Tommy had enough sense not to say something really stupid to Lionel about civil rights.

However, she pushed that possible problem aside when, to her delight, Mr. Kyle put her and Kevin in the same group. Unfortunately, he'd also put Bridget there. Wendy tried to ignore the big smile the Irish girl had for Kevin when she heard her name called. She didn't much like that Kevin had returned the smile, but then he *had* smiled at her too. Wendy flailed around in her purse, pretending to look for a pen. She had to get a grip since they were going to be working on the project together.

The fourth person to join their group was Dwayne Bernard. He was another new student. His parents had moved to Middletown last spring and opened a car dealership, but Dwayne hadn't enrolled in their local school until this fall, apparently finishing his junior year in Minneapolis. He was tall and lanky with pale skin and dyed-black hair that just barely met the dress code. He looked older than eighteen, but maybe that was because he usually wore black and was so quiet. No one really knew much about him.

"I am verra happy the teacher put us together," Bridget said, supposedly to all of them, but her eyes rested on Kevin.

"I think we'll be a good team," he answered. "Wendy and I worked on a similar project last year, so that should help."

Wendy almost gloated that Kevin had pointed that out, but Bridget smiled at her guilelessly. "Then I hope ye will help me too. I want to be friends."

Whoosh. Wendy's little inflated moment of ego went flat. How could she not like Bridget? The girl was *nice.*

"Ye will probably find this project a bit different from how we do things in Ireland," Kevin said to Bridget.

"I've already noticed some things this fall," she answered, "but I'm glad ye are here to help me sort it through."

"Any time." Kevin turned to Dwayne. "I'm Kevin O'Keefe. Glad to be working with ye as well."

Dwayne studied him as though he were some sort of strange specimen under a microscope. For a moment, Wendy thought he was going to be rude and not answer, but he finally gave a short nod. "Dwayne." Then he turned his attention away.

A puzzled expression crossed Kevin's face and then quickly vanished. Wendy looked at Dwayne. Quiet wasn't really the right word for him, she thought as she watched him look above the heads of the other students to gaze at what looked like an ordinary wall to her. Aloof might be a better word.

A lot of the kids thought he was stuck-up because he kept to himself and didn't mingle. Since he drove a fancy new car, they also thought he felt he was too good for country kids, but Wendy felt a little sorry for him. The kids—even the twins—generally left him alone. Government was the only class she had with him and, until now, she hadn't really talked to him much either, since he preferred to sit in the far back corner. Did he really like being by himself so much?

Maybe by working with him in this group she could get him to overcome whatever was causing him to be so withdrawn. Help him to fit in. At the very least, "helping" Dwayne would keep Wendy's mind off the fact that Kevin would be "helping" Bridget.

It seemed like a grown-up thing to do.

****

Dwayne let himself into his empty house, tossed his books into a corner, and took the stairs two at a time to his room. Once there, he bolted the door even though he knew no one was home—were his parents ever home?—and walked to his dresser. Digging through his sock drawer, he breathed a sigh of relief when his fingers touched the small plastic case pushed to the back.

He opened it, carefully taking out one of the three Quaaludes he had left and popped it. He'd have to make some excuse to go to Mankato this weekend to see his dealer for more. He'd been lucky to meet the guy while in rehab last spring or else he would have had to drive all the way to the Twin Cities to get his drugs. Easier to make excuses to his parents about trips to 'Kato. At least one good thing about having absentee parents was they didn't question him how he spent the generous allowance they gave him—which they probably did so he wouldn't bug them about anything.

Dwayne flopped into a chair, closed his eyes, and waited for the drug to take its hold. He preferred pot since it was easier to come by, but the smell of weed was too hard to get rid of. His mother—when she could tear herself away from her art studio—probably wouldn't notice since the oils and turpentine she used had their own effect, but his dad had a nose like a bloodhound—and a heavy fist.

He tried not to think about Government class today. Why in hell had the teacher put him in a *group*? He didn't do well in groups. He'd proved that point when the counselors in rehab put him in with others for therapy. He'd gotten into fights with the ones who acted like they knew more than him. Bunch of idiots. Had none of them ever tripped on acid? On the really good stuff? That's when the *real* world was revealed—not just lights and colors and sounds, but the universe opened up. Knowledge that couldn't be perceived by the normal human brain was unveiled to him. He knew things and understood things those stupid counselors didn't get.

He was smarter than they were, but they wouldn't admit it. When he'd told them he could see where they'd hidden microphones in the therapy room, they'd denied it. When he said the man on the loudspeaker had warned him, they would deny it, saying there was no loudspeaker. He'd *heard* it, plain as day, but he'd been put in a damn straitjacket and a shrink had given him a shot of something that made everything look gray.

And now he was supposed to work with three kids who acted like they'd been living on Gilligan's Island too long? His prescription for chlorpromazine was barely strong enough to keep him quiet in class. He'd managed by sitting in corners, focusing on blank walls, and avoiding interaction. His father had already warned that another irrational outburst was going to get him sent to a mental ward instead of rehab. Of course, his father didn't understand that what he called irrational outbursts were actually an effort to enlighten others. He was smarter than any person he knew, but they were all too stupid to appreciate that.

Dwayne sighed as the hypnotic quality of the pill began to take over. He was content in his little cocoon and able to make it through the day until he could get home to his 'ludes. Right now he had no choice but to keep up pretenses and tolerate the other students.

But work in a group? He wasn't sure if he could.

Maybe he needed to see if his dealer could get him some speed, too. It intensified everything.

Chapter Four

"If only human females were as easy to understand as ye four-legged ones." Kevin finished feeding James' mare later that afternoon, gave her a final pat, and headed back to the Lambarts' farmhouse, pondering what to do about Bridget.

After Government class, she'd hung around, clearly wanting to talk, while he had had plans to walk with Wendy to the bus. That didn't happen. Although their situations weren't the same, Bridget reminded him too much of his sister to just abandon her, so he'd lingered in the school hall listening to her until he almost missed their bus.

It felt strange not having James around, since they'd established a brotherly bond almost immediately last year, but at least he knew the Lambarts, and that familiarity helped. It wasn't so easy for Bridget. He had absolutely no idea of how to get her to overcome her homesickness. He had quickly grown to like everything about America, or at least Minnesota. The rural farming community wasn't so different from the Irish countryside, except there were cattle and not sheep in the pastures. And barb-wire fences instead of rock ones. But the people were open and friendly and he'd felt comfortable early on. Bridget had grown up in Dublin, not far from the River Liffey and close to Trinity College. Her parents were both professors who thought she'd benefit from spending a year in a foreign school system. She didn't want to disappoint them, so she always wrote that she was loving everything. Except she wasn't.

And somehow, in a brief two days, she'd managed to make him feel partially responsible for changing that. He was pretty sure part of the reason he was feeling this way was guilt over leaving his own family after his father died. His mother had assured him that if she needed help, his uncles and her own brothers were practically within shouting distance since they all lived close by. And Mary had lots of female aunts and cousins too. Still. He'd been torn between returning to a country he'd been drawn to or staying home.

Mrs. Lambart must have noticed his pensive mood when he sat down at the dinner table because she gave him a quizzical look.

"Did things not go well at school today?"

"Things were fine. I'll be workin' on a group project in Government that deals with all the unrest that's happenin' here in America," Kevin replied. "I am guessin' I'll be doin' a lot of comparison to the Irish troubles, too."

"It's almost as if we're waiting for a time bomb to go off that will change us forever," Mr. Lambart said.

"It's true there's unease in the world," his wife answered, "but I don't think it's quite that serious."

"No? The war's escalating in Asia with no end in sight, last spring a military coup in Greece forced the king out, Israel launched preemptive strikes on the Arabs this summer, Russia is rattling sabers at China, not to mention the trouble brewing in Ireland—"

"Enough of such talk," Mrs. Lambart interjected.

"It's bad enough watching it on the television. Let's not upset our digestion at the table." She turned to Kevin. "Who's working on this project with you? Maybe Wendy?"

Kevin hoped he wasn't blushing. He hated when he did that. But Mrs. Lambart had been aware of his puppy-dog interest in Wendy last year. "Aye. There's four of us," he said before she could comment. "a guy and another foreign exchange student."

"That would be the young lady the Hoffmans are hosting?" Mrs. Lambart asked.

"Aye. Her name's Bridget McBride."

"And from Ireland too?" Mr. Lambart asked. "You must have a lot in common."

"Well, sure," Kevin said, "except she's homesick and I'm not."

"Ah, the poor thing," Mrs. Lambart said. "It can't be too enjoyable living with the Hoffmans. They took the death of their son Billy so hard."

"And they're not young either, having had Billy late," Mr. Lambart added.

His wife nodded. "She's probably lonely, rattling around in that big house with no young people around."

"I suppose that's part of it." Kevin hadn't really thought about that since he had a brother and sister and lots of relatives."

"Well, invite her over to have dinner with us one night," Mr. Lambart said.

Kevin was pretty sure that wasn't a good idea, if only because Bridget—or Wendy—might get the wrong idea. "I don't think—"

"I have a thought." Mrs. Lambart tilted her head. "Why don't you invite both Wendy and Bridget over for dinner? That'll give the girls a chance to talk and become friends."

That didn't sound like a good idea either, but before Kevin could say so, Mr. Lambart interceded. "Splendid. With James off to college, we could use some young people around here. How about Friday?"

Kevin grasped for a straw. "I think there's a basketball game that night."

"Yes, there probably is," Mrs. Lambart replied. "Next week, then. All right?"

Reluctantly, Kevin nodded. He couldn't refuse his host parents, but he hoped his own troubles weren't just beginning.

****

"Did you ever wish you'd tried out for cheerleader?" Jo asked Wendy as they climbed onto the bleachers in the school gym for the Friday night basketball game.

"No." Wendy watched the six girls in their purple-and-white uniforms hopping up and down as though they were trying to get out of a fire-ant bed. "I'm not the type."

Jo settled on the seat. "What do you mean by that?"

"Oh, you know. The type that's really popular."

"Everyone likes you."

"My *friends* like me," Wendy answered. "Cheerleaders have to be voted in by the whole student body."

Jo smiled. "Well, you *know* the whole student body. It's not a city school like Brooklyn was."

"That must really be something. How many girls try out? Over a hundred?"

"Probably. The administration narrows it down, though. They have to kind of audition in front of a faculty committee to show they can do the routines and jumps and stuff. Then the student body votes. The top twenty-five do their routines in front of everyone and the kids vote again." Jo shrugged. "It's kind of like politics. They even campaign with posters and things."

"Wow. All that matters here is if you're pretty and flirty." Wendy gave her a wry smile. "I'm not either one."

"You're cute."

Wendy shook her head. "Maybe in a wholesome kind of way."

"Wholesome?"

"That's what Mary Anne called me last year when she got back from San Francisco. She said I was refreshing, like a kid sister should be."

"For Mary Anne, that's a compliment."

Wendy grimaced. "*Wholesome* and *refreshing* aren't exactly what make guys get in line for the next dance."

Jo gave her a questioning look. "I thought you didn't like to dance."

"I don't." Her cousin was being literal again. "I meant… Oh, never mind."

She wasn't about to admit she was a little jealous of how pretty Bridget was. Or that she had a way of getting Kevin's attention. Not that she flirted. It was more like being helpless and needy, two things Wendy couldn't pull off even if she tried.

"Kevin just came in." Jo broke her melancholy reverie. "Tim and Tommy are with him."

Wendy looked over at the side door as the three made their way toward the bleachers. Carla and Susan were pom-pom girls, so they wouldn't be sitting with them. She wondered if Bridget would be coming. She hadn't attended any football games last fall, probably because the Hoffmans didn't go, but she had shown up for a couple of basketball games before Christmas.

"Let me get their attention," Jo said as she waved. One of the twins waved back. Kevin looked up.

Jo nudged her. "Wave at him."

"I don't want to look like…" Her words were lost as Jo pushed her elbow up. For a moment her hand flopped in the air like a washrag being shaken out before she managed some semblance of control. "Geez, Jo. He'll think I'm spastic."

Jo looked unperturbed. "At least he saw you."

Wendy didn't answer as the guys climbed up to join them, Tommy in the lead with Kevin behind him and Tim trailing behind since he'd stopped to wave at Carla. Luckily there was plenty of room, even if Bridget showed up. As selfish as it was, Wendy hoped she'd stay home.

They'd fallen into a sort of routine this past week. Kevin joined her and Jo for lunch, but so did Bridget. Tim and Tommy sat at their table too since Carla and Susan had different lunch schedules. That meant the conversation stayed general.

Government class was even worse. Mr. Kyle was a stickler for a seating chart unless they were working in groups, which would only happen once a week. That meant Wendy sat with one twin behind her and the other beside her while Kevin and Bridget sat near the door. Luckily, Mr. Kyle was also a stickler for no talking during class.

That left a few minutes after school before the buses left to be able to talk, and lots of kids hung out on the sidewalk. Maybe next week would be better.

"Hey," Tommy said as he reached their bench and started to sit down beside Wendy.

He didn't quite make it as Jo reached across and grabbed his arm, giving him a sharp tug that almost sent him sprawling. He gave her an indignant look, but she only smiled.

"I want to talk to you."

"Jeepers. You don't have to knock me over."

Wendy wasn't sure whether she should be mortified at the obvious move that left the seat next to her vacant for Kevin or amused at her cousin's boldness. In either case, it had the desired effect. Kevin sat down beside her, his thigh brushing hers briefly.

For a moment it seemed like every nerve ending tingled. This was as close as Wendy had been to him since he'd gotten back. She could feel his body heat after having climbed the bleachers. His hair was tousled from being outside, the stubborn lock falling forward. She fought an urge to brush it back just so she could touch him. A subtle scent of soap and cologne clung to him as well and made Wendy think of galloping their horses across open fields with the wind in their faces. Maybe as soon as some of the snow melted…

"Don't sit there!" Tommy said to his twin as Tim reached them. "Unless you want Jo to tackle you."

"What?"

Tim looked puzzled. Wendy felt like her face was on fire. He glanced at Kevin and then gave her a knowing look. "Need to leave the lovebirds alone?"

The tips of Kevin's ears turned pink and Wendy considered tripping Tim and watching him somersault down the rows of bleachers, but she managed to keep both feet on the floor. She didn't want to kill him, but a good trouncing would have been very satisfactory.

"Just go. The game's about to start."

Tim wiggled his brows and grinned. "I think it already has."

Her face flamed again and this time she lifted her foot, but Tim, sensing revenge, had already slipped past her.

She gave his back a menacing look and turned her attention to the floor as the cheerleaders began a chant as the team finished its warm-ups. A moment later everyone stood as the first notes of "The Star-Spangled Banner" sounded.

As she listened to the anthem, Wendy detected a slight movement by the gym door. Glancing over, she saw Bridget had just come in.

Once the song was finished, she would be joining them. And, unfortunately, the seat on the other side of Kevin was vacant. Just her luck.

****

Bridget gave them all a big smile as she climbed the bleachers. When she arrived, she told them, "I've always liked basketball. My parents let me see the games at Trinity College."

"Irish college ball is a wee bit different from American high school, nae?" Kevin moved to allow room for Bridget to sit. As he did, his thigh brushed Wendy's again. It had the effect of touching metal after walking across wool carpet. The shock sent a tingle up his thigh along with an urge to press closer to her. He quickly shifted position. Once could be considered accidental. Twice within a few minutes would make Wendy think he was coming on way too fast. He didn't want to make any mistakes this time around.

Wendy's leg moved too, although he wasn't sure if it was toward him or not.

"It would be nice if we'd qualify for State our senior year," she said.

"Is the team that good?" Bridget asked. "I can't tell."

While Wendy answered her, Kevin let his thoughts drift. He'd told his brother about Wendy when he'd gone home and Ian had insisted that girls didn't like guys who wore their hearts on the sleeves. He'd even winked and suggested playing hard to get and making Wendy chase him. Kevin wasn't too sure about that tactic, although it certainly seemed to work for his brother, who had several girls calling him every week.

However, he was determined, this year, that he wasn't going to trail after Wendy like a lost sheep, or worse, act like a wolf and make her feel she was his prey. He would adhere to his seafaring grandfather's old adage of "steady as she goes" which he used to say when teaching Kevin how to sail. He would hold his ship—or in this case, himself—on a straight course. No putting the proverbial rail-in-the-water or luffing his sails either. So to speak. He would reach his goal by proceeding in a slow, methodical fashion to make sure they were true friends first.

A shout went up from the stands as one of the players made a long shot from center court that went through the basket just before the buzzer sounded for the first quarter's end.

"What a lucky shot!" Tommy said.

"Maybe the luck had something to do with our Irish friends sitting here." Tim leaned forward. "You know what they say about the luck of the Irish."

Kevin suppressed a groan. The twins made random remarks like that, thinking they were funny, he supposed. Last year, they'd made remarks about pots of gold at the end of rainbows and catching leprechauns.

"Luck has nothing to do with it," Wendy said as though she'd read his mind. "Doug Finley is just a really good shot."

"Finley is an Irish name," Bridget said. "Is he a foreign exchange student too?"

Wendy shook her head. "No, his family has been here forever. He started bouncing a basketball when he was in the first grade, though."

She was speaking of the guy who was the shooting guard and a junior. Just mentioning how long he'd been practicing made Kevin realize how well all the students knew each other and reminded him he was the *outlier,* not only by nationality but also by time. Villagers in Ireland were still close-knit like this, too, many of them able to trace their ancestries back to Irish clans and some even to medieval kings.

Middletown was a bit like that, many of the families having come from Europe in the early 1800s to farm the fertile black soil. They kept to a lot of German and Scandinavian traditions, with a few Scots-Irish thrown in. Maybe that was why he liked it here. Would Wendy be willing to accept that he hadn't lived here "forever," as she put it?

Kevin sighed. He was getting way ahead of himself. While he might not be overly superstitious, no one with an ounce of Irish blood would deny the Fae. Just in case a fairie or two were about.

He would work on being friends first. But he fervently hoped by prom time in May, the Fae—if a faerie were listening—would be smiling on him.

Chapter Five

"What's that?" Wendy asked Kevin after they'd finished lunch on Monday and he took a brown envelope from his binder.

"Information from Notre Dame," Kevin replied. "I requested it back in December once I knew for sure I'd be comin' back here."

"You're thinking about going there because they're the Fighting Irish?" Tim asked. "They're not really Irish, you know."

"And there are no girls," Tommy added.

"I know," Kevin answered, apparently to both questions. "But they've got a good journalism program."

Wendy gave him a surprised look. "You want to be a journalist?"

Kevin nodded. "I like findin' out what the facts really are. It's why I like our government project."

Bridget shook her head. "But reportin' the facts can be dangerous. We've already had reporters hurt in North Ireland."

"People wouldn't know what's really going on with the IRA and Fianna Fáil if reporters didn't get in there."

"Aye, but remember what happened when Queen Elizabeth was nearly killed in Belfast in 1966," Bridget said. "The nationalist reporters from Dublin who'd covered the Queen's openin' of the bridge became targets as well."

"And if they had nae been there, vigilante justice might have been done to the worker who threw the brick off the scaffoldin'," Kevin replied. "He got his just punishment, but it was done in a court of law."

"We've certainly got our share of problems over here too," Jo said. "Practically every week people get hurt in civil rights protests."

Lionel looked up from his plate. "No one would get hurt if black people were given the rights they deserve."

Wendy gave him an apprehensive glance. Had he actually taken part in last summer's riots in Detroit? Although he wasn't argumentative, he did seem to be defensive sometimes. She didn't know if that was normal or not. "Well, Dr. King is working to gets those rights without violence."

"'Tis reporters who help your Martin Luther King get his message out, nae?" Kevin asked. "And also cover the riots?"

"And they get hurt too," Bridget replied before Lionel could. "'Tis dangerous."

He shrugged and went back to eating. Wendy frowned. "I hadn't thought of it that way. The reporters *are* in the thick of it, aren't they?"

"Yeah, well. Kevin could also get famous," Tommy said. "Just look at Walter Cronkite."

"And Huntley-Brinkley," Tim added.

Kevin smiled. "I want to get out and get the facts. Ye don't have to be famous to do that."

"Kind of like that photo in the paper about Vietnam," Jo said. "Hardly anyone looks to see who the photographers are, and they're right in the line of fire."

"'Tis their job, though. They are doin' what they need to do." Kevin turned back to his papers. "Anyway,

I think the University of Notre Dame du Lac will give me the best trainin'.'"

"*Du lac*?" Wendy asked. "Doesn't that mean 'the lake' in French?"

"Aye. 'Tis actually 'Our Lady of the Lake' in English."

Wendy felt her eyes widen. "Like in Camelot!"

Kevin looked confused. "Camelot? Ye mean the King Arthur legend?"

"Yes! The Lady of the Lake raised Lancelot to become Arthur's greatest knight," Wendy answered.

Jo gave her a side glance. "Except for the cheating part."

"I don't mean that. Lancelot helped Arthur win lots of battles. If it hadn't been for him, Arthur might not have defeated the Saxons—"

"Geez, you act like he's *real*," Tim said.

"*Camelot* was a movie, remember?" Tommy asked.

Tim grinned. "Based on *myth*."

"Was it?" Wendy shot back. "There's lots of nonfiction out there that says King Arthur was real. So who's to say Lancelot wasn't real too." She made a face at her cousins as they started to laugh. "My point is that maybe Notre Dame du Lac—Our Lady of the Lake—can make Kevin the greatest reporter ever, just like Lancelot was the greatest knight!"

She stopped suddenly, feeling her face heat as everyone gaped at her. Good golly, she sounded silly. Even worse, she sounded like she had a real crush on Kevin. His face had even turned pink. She was going to die of mortification. Right now.

"I'll settle for good," Kevin said, "but who knows? With a leprechaun for a mascot, anything can happen, nae?"

"That's true." Jo gave the twins a stern look. "Have either of you thought about what you might want to do?"

"Sure," they answered in unison.

"Go to college. Join a frat," Tim said.

Tommy grinned. "And party."

Jo rolled her eyes. "Why am I not surprised?"

Bridget frowned. "*Nach bhfuil admhálacha eile agat?*"

The twins stared. "Huh?" Tommy asked.

Tim looked confused. "What did you say?"

A stricken expression crossed Bridget's face and she looked at Kevin. He raised one brow and then shrugged. "She asked if you don't have any other aspirations."

Jo laughed. "Good one, Bridget."

"Now just a minute…" Tommy sputtered.

Tim joined him in protesting and Wendy was grateful the attention had been diverted from her disastrous declaration. She'd all but admitted she was smitten with Kevin. She'd have to guard what she said from now on if she didn't want the twins making life a living torture chamber.

But…secretly, she thought Kevin's ambition made him as knightly as any of King Arthur's men.

****

As Kevin walked into Government class seconds before the bell rang, he was still chortling over Bridget's outburst at lunch. He had been surprised that she'd spoken up, although her lapse into Gaelic probably meant she had been truly incredulous over the twins' idea of college, since her own parents taught at Trinity. She'd apologized to Tim and Tommy—which Kevin didn't think was necessary since they'd acted like dorks—but the whole incident had taken the attention away from Wendy. He was pretty sure her outburst hadn't been intended either.

She didn't really think of him as a knight, did she? His impulse to laugh disappeared. He was no gallant knight. Worse, though, if she thought of him as one meant she didn't see him for who he was. Instead, she'd have some romantic notions of how he was *supposed* to act. And he didn't want to *act*. He wanted Wendy to like him for himself, nor did he want to worship her from afar, as knights did their ladies.

However, he suspected all of this was going to be a big muddle if he actually asked her for a date anytime soon. He sighed. Better to stick with his original idea of becoming friends first and not giving any indication he wanted her to be his girl.

"You just barely made it," Bridget said as he took the empty seat at their project table. "I was getting worried."

Kevin noticed Wendy shot her a quick glance, but she didn't say anything. He'd noticed that she often watched Bridget and, while she was polite, she wasn't quite as open and friendly as she was with others. She'd turned away just now to give Dwayne some notes. Bridget didn't seem to notice, but it reminded Kevin that Mrs. Lambart expected him to invite both Bridget and Wendy to dinner.

"I got stuck talking to my shop teacher." Kevin produced a piece of green paper. "He gave me a tardy excuse, just in case."

"Oh, good," Bridget answered. "Better not to take chances."

Dwayne diverted his attention to her for a moment.

"Taking chances is the only way to experience life." Then he returned his gaze to the wall behind Kevin.

Strange bloke, that one. Last week, when they'd been assigned to work together, he hadn't uttered a single word beyond giving his name. Kevin had an instinctive distrust of people who were too quiet and withdrawn, but perhaps that was because the Irish were gregarious by nature. Or perhaps he'd been seeing too many spaghetti westerns like *The Good, The Bad and The Ugly*. He loved American movies and television and cowboy boots. Dwayne reminded him a little of Lee Van Cleef's character, or maybe Anthony Perkins in that horror film.

Kevin abruptly pushed those thoughts away. James had teased him last year about getting too wrapped up in the movies. He had no justification for thinking such negative things. Wendy sure wouldn't think of him as knightly and he could almost hear Bridget lapsing into Gaelic: *Ná bí ag iarraidh trioblóde*...don't go looking for trouble.

Which brought his thoughts full circle. He still had to issue that invitation for dinner.

Maybe later.

****

"It was so nice of you to invite us over for dinner," Jo told Mrs. Lambart on Thursday evening after they'd been seated at the dinner table.

"We like having young people around," Mrs. Lambart answered. "Once James left for college and before Kevin arrived, Mr. Lambart and I just sort of rattled around in the house."

Wendy thought of how ironic it was that she was dining in the Lambarts' home. Last year, when she'd been besotted with James, she would have nearly killed for such an opportunity. She certainly would have seen it as a step toward a relationship.

She glanced covertly at Kevin. This invitation could hardly be seen as such a step. Kevin had invited her and Bridget, as well as Jo, at the same time and he'd made it pretty clear it was Mrs. Lambart's idea.

"Kevin tells me you are working on a term project, pertaining to subcultures, for Government class." Mrs. Lambart passed a bowl of mashed potatoes. "That sounds interesting."

"I'm not," Jo answered, "since I have a different class period."

"Dwayne Bernard is the fourth person in our group," Wendy said.

"Bernard?" Mr. Lambart asked. "Is he the son of the new car dealer who moved here last year?"

"Yes," Wendy replied, "but Dwayne just enrolled this year."

"Is he the one who drives around in that new red Camaro?" Mrs. Lambart picked up the gravy dish and started it around. "I don't think we've ever seen him out of the car."

"He kind of sticks to himself," Jo said.

"Maybe he's just shy," Mrs. Lambart said, "being in a new school and all."

Was that Dwayne's problem? Wendy wasn't sure, but it sounded possible. She'd tried to study him Monday afternoon while they worked on their project, but he had remained aloof. The only time he'd looked interested in anything she said was when she mentioned that Timothy Leary's doctoral dissertation was on social dimensions of personality. And the only reason she'd known *that* was because of the similar project James and Mary Anne had done last year.

At least it had gotten Dwayne to say that Harvard should have allowed Dr. Leary to continue his research and experiments. Kevin had argued that the trials with psychedelic drugs had proved too unstable to continue—he'd helped work on James and Mary Anne's project too—and Dwayne had shrugged and gone back to staring at the wall.

Perhaps she should do more research on the whole topic if it would get Dwayne to participate and get involved. And her mother always said complimenting a person helped the person's self-esteem. Wendy could work on that.

"It does take a little time to adjust," Jo said, "especially if he's used to a big city."

"Being in a new school is hard. Maybe Dwayne misses his old friends." Bridget smiled at Kevin. "It helps when there's someone familiar from home."

"Of course it does," Mrs. Lambart said. "And you're welcome to come visit any time, Bridget. I'm sure Kevin would like to reminisce about Ireland without boring his other friends."

"I'm sure none of us would be bored talking about Ireland," Wendy blurted before she thought. Her face heated as she realized she must have sounded petulant.

Jo shot a quick glance at her. "Actually, wouldn't Ireland fit into your research project? You're studying Civil Rights protests too, aren't you?"

"Yes, we are." Wendy was going to give Jo a big hug later for that save. "We could expand that to include what's going on in Northern Ireland as well."

Kevin nodded. "There are certainly some similarities."

"Mr. Kyle did mention anti-war protesters going to Canada," Wendy added, "so he didn't limit us just to the United States."

"There you go, then," Jo said. "I think learning about Ireland would be interesting too, and I'm not even involved in your project."

Wendy was going to owe her cousin big time for coming up with that idea. She didn't dare look at her, though, because her expression would give her away. She didn't want Bridget coming over to the Lambarts' to spend time with Kevin.

"Of course, it would be an excellent opportunity for all of you," Mrs. Lambart said, "but I know the Hoffmans don't have any other young people at their place either, so if you ever get lonely, Bridget, you can come visit Kevin and us."

"Thank ye! I'd like to do that." Bridget beamed at them. "I appreciate how nice everyone is, but it still helps to talk to someone from home. Nae, Kevin?"

Wendy kept her eyes down, not wanting to hear his answer. There was a long pause and she fought the urge to look up.

"Aye," Kevin finally said.

"Good! Then it's settled." Mrs. Lambart rose. "Now who wants dessert?"

The last thing Wendy wanted to think about was dessert. It seemed Bridget had already gotten hers.

Chapter Six

Wendy and Jo tried not to get slush on their boots as they waited for the school bus Thursday afternoon. Thanks to a mid-January thaw, everything was muddy. Wendy just hoped the twins weren't going to do something childish like stomp in the puddles and spray everyone.

Tommy squinted up at the sky. "If this mild weather holds out, maybe we can take the horses out this weekend. Tim and I are bored out of our trees being stuck in."

"Yeah, good idea," Tim said. "Susan and Carla are going shopping for the Valentine dance, so we're free."

Jo nodded. "I know Silver really could use the exercise."

Silver was Luke's young Andalusian that they were boarding while he was away in college. The horse was spirited and pretty much allowed only Luke or Jo to ride him, which was fine with Wendy. She had no desire to land on her rump. Her own horse was older and more settled. "Jupiter probably would like to get out too."

Jo gave her a side look. "I'll bet James' horse could use some exercise as well."

Tim laughed. "Is that your way of suggesting we invite Kevin to ride with us and Wendy?"

"Yeah, I think Wendy could use a little help," Tommy said.

"With what?" Wendy hoped her face didn't look as red as it felt. Maybe she could sidetrack the twins. "I'm perfectly capable of handling my own horse, thank you."

Tommy grinned. "Don't even try changing the subject. We're not talking about Jupiter."

"Well, I don't want to talk about…anything else." Wendy looked down the street. Where was that stupid school bus anyway?

"Ah, come on, cuz. Kevin's been back three weeks and he hasn't even asked you out," Tim said.

Tommy nodded. "A little matchmaking on our part won't hurt—"

"Don't you *dare*!" Wendy turned on both of them. "Just mind your own business."

Tim looked at Tommy. "I'd say she's a little touchy on the subject."

Tommy affected a thoughtful expression. "Probably because—"

"Because *nothing*!" Wendy somehow refrained from shouting the words. "Just stay out of it."

"Because of Bridget," Tim continued as though she hadn't said a word.

"Okay, you two. Just stop it," Jo said. "I'm sorry I even mentioned inviting Kevin."

Tim shook his head. "No, it was a good idea. Kevin needs a little encouragement, that's all."

"Or maybe you could make him jealous, cuz," Tommy said. "It works both ways, you know."

"I will *not*…" Wendy stopped abruptly as Kevin came down the steps toward them. She prayed he hadn't overheard any of the stupid conversation. She would simply die on the spot if he had. She managed a quick, sideways glance at him. He looked unperturbed, so maybe all was well.

The school bus finally came lumbering along and rolled to a stop. Wendy breathed a sigh of relief as she climbed on, but it was short-lived.

"We can make it happen for you," Tommy said from behind her.

"We'll be glad to spread a few rumors to make him jealous," Tim added in a whisper.

Wendy chose to ignore both of them, although she could practically hear them snickering. If she could only appear casual and unconcerned, by morning some other scheme would have diverted them.

She hoped.

****

Two semi-miracles occurred by Saturday. The temperatures stayed above freezing, allowing more snow to melt, and the twins' girlfriends decided they needed to go shopping with them.

Which left Wendy free to ride with Kevin without Tim and Tommy hovering like hawks.

"I really don't mind staying home," Jo said for the zillionth time as they waited near the barn for Kevin to arrive.

"You're coming with us," Wendy answered. "No more arguing about it."

"But it will give you a chance to finally be alone with Kevin," Jo protested.

"And he'll think I connived the whole thing to do just that," Wendy replied.

"I doubt it, but even if he did, what's the problem? Maybe you need to let Kevin know how much you like him."

Wendy shook her head. "He should tell me first."

Jo shook her head too. "I keep telling you we aren't living in the Fifties anymore. Girls are going to ask guys to the Valentine's dance."

Wendy refrained from rolling her eyes. "That's because it's a *Sadie Hawkins* dance. Girls are supposed to do the asking."

"Don't forget this is also a leap year," Jo said. "That means girls can do the asking for the *entire* year."

Wendy stuck out her chin. "You didn't ask Luke out first."

"No, but I did follow him to that hidden cave across from the old bridge—"

"And nearly drowned when it splintered and you fell into the river."

Jo smiled, her face turning pink. "And Luke saved my life."

Wendy remembered how Luke had brought her cousin home and carried her into the house wrapped in his jacket. "Well, I'm not planning to put myself into harm's way to find out if Kevin would do the same."

"Silly. I wasn't suggesting you do," Jo said. "I certainly didn't *plan* to fall into the water. Anyway, we're not talking life and death here. You and Kevin could go for a nice, private ride—"

"No."

"Something tells me there's another reason you're being so stubborn about this." Jo tilted her head, studying her. "Spill it."

Wendy started to deny it, then paused. "There is something. But you have to swear to secrecy if I tell you."

"Of course I will."

She hesitated a moment longer. "You remember

when Kevin went back to Ireland last year, he left me a letter?"

Jo smiled. "Which you wouldn't let anyone read."

"That's because he chewed me out."

Jo's eyes widened like owls. "He did *what*? I can't believe he would put you down in any way."

"Well, maybe not putting me down, but he did reprimand me like I was a child and he was the adult."

Jo drew her brows together. "What did he say?"

She paused again, reliving her embarrassment. "He basically told me I was making a fool of myself for trailing after James when he was only interested in Mary Anne."

"Ah—"

"I know. I know. He was right. I finally saw that for myself." Wendy grimaced. "I'm not going to make that mistake again by running after another guy."

"But Kevin doesn't have eyes for anyone—"

"No? What about Bridget? She's *always* around."

"What do you expect him to do? Tell her she can't hang out with us?"

Wendy gave her cousin a mulish look. "That would be a start."

"You know very well Kevin's too much of a gentleman to do that." Jo laid a hand on Wendy's arm. "He's the kind of person that, if you *did* fall into the river, he'd jump in to save you."

"He'd probably do that for anyone," Wendy muttered as she scuffed her boot in the dirt.

Her cousin smiled again. "Well, you did say you wanted a knight."

Jo was right, blast it. Knights were supposed to be courtly. To everyone.

"And here comes Sir Galahad now." Jo pointed down the road.

Wendy looked up to see Kevin cantering James' sorrel up the long driveway, and she blinked. The noon sun glinted off the horse's reddish coat and the russet color of his deerskin jacket. It also caught the coppery color of Kevin's hair, giving him the appearance of a fiery avenger. For a moment she half-expected to see a flaming sword in one hand. And then he passed beneath the shade of several oaks lining the drive and she blinked again, the image gone, and he was just plain Kevin.

But maybe a little bit Sir Galahad, too.

****

"No Smothers Brothers today?" Kevin asked as Jo and Wendy mounted and the three of them started toward the main road.

Jo laughed. "Too bad Tim's name really isn't Dick. Then that description would be one hundred percent accurate."

"It's pretty accurate as it is," Wendy said, "except they probably don't get into as much trouble as the twins do."

"Not sure about that," Jo said. "Some of their political comments are pretty controversial."

"Well, it does seem like America has gotten more divided since last year when I was here," Kevin said. "The anti-war crowd is larger and more vocal and the Civil Rights protestors are more violent."

'It's kind of like the nation is being divided, isn't it?" Jo asked. "You either have to be for the war or against it. You either think everyone should have equal rights or you don't. And people can't seem to agree with each other on anything."

"'Tis almost the same in Ireland," Kevin said. "The nationalists really want Northern Ireland to join the Republic and the young, educated Catholics who aren't gettin' jobs up there have formed a Civil Rights organization that, when I left, was plannin' a big march from Belfast to Derry. With all the unrest, I'm afraid 'twill turn violent like the riots here do."

"One more reason I'm glad I live in Middletown," Jo said. "Pretty much, we all get along here."

"Aye, but even in small towns like this, change is happenin'. Look at how many new students ye have this year." Kevin grinned. "Nae includin' Bridget and meself of course."

Wendy didn't much like that reference. It made them sound like a *couple*. She shot Jo a "*See what I mean?*" look, but her cousin subtly shook her head.

"I guess Bob Dylan was right," she said. "The times they are a-changin'."

Jo either didn't connect Wendy's glare to their earlier conversation while they were waiting for Kevin or she chose to ignore it. Probably the last. It still irritated Wendy. But it was too nice a day to spoil with a foul mood, so she decided to change the subject.

"Did anyone last year show you the secret cave where Mary Anne and Jo were taken when they were kidnapped?"

Kevin gave her a startled look. "Kidnapped?"

"Well, *I* wasn't, really," Jo said. "Mary Anne was the one who was abducted."

"Here? In Middletown?"

"Right here," Wendy answered. "I guess that just shows these things can happen anywhere."

"Tell me."

Wendy filled him in on what led up to the kidnapping, as they walked their horses down the gravel road toward the river. Jo filled in what happened once she'd been caught and taken to the cave too.

"And Luke rescued us by using his tracking skills," Jo finished as they stopped by the old splintered bridge across from the cave.

"Tracking skills?" Kevin asked. "Like in the Western movies?"

"Kind of." Jo smiled. "Luke's part Ojibwa. His dad made him go to Native American cultural camps when he was a kid."

"Interesting," Kevin said. "My parents made me learn Gaelic and spend time on the Dingle peninsula where a lot of the Celtic culture remains. I guess 'tis kind of the same thing."

Wendy nodded. "I think that's why the Black Power movement is growing so fast."

"Probably," Jo said. "Preserving our heritages is important, but we should use them to better understand each other."

"Right now, it seems to be havin' the opposite effect, though." Kevin frowned. "Just look at our Government class. Hardly anyone talks to Lionel. Dwayne sticks to himself. Bridget is homesick because she doesn't feel she fits in—"

"Maybe Mr. Kyle should make it mandatory we all watch *Star Trek*." Wendy didn't want to hear about Bridget. "The crew on the *Enterprise* are all different, yet they get along."

Kevin gave her a thoughtful look. Wendy wasn't sure if he thought she'd cut him off because he mentioned Bridget…which she *did*. Or if he thought she was a complete airhead. She wasn't sure which was worse. How embarrassing. Her cheeks warmed.

"I meant…"

"Nae need to explain." He held up a hand. "Lots of lessons could be learned from that show. Maybe we could use some of that for our project."

Wendy breathed a sigh of relief, while Jo gave her an odd look. No doubt she'd get scolded later, but for now Jo had turned her attention back to the cave, which was mostly hidden from their view by boulders and bramble.

"I haven't been up there since the incident," she said.

"There is nae need to go now," Kevin responded with a quick glance at each of them. "'Tis perhaps better to leave some things alone."

Jo nodded. "Perhaps you are right."

As they turned their horses around to head home, Wendy wasn't sure if his remark about leaving things alone was directed at Jo or at her.

Chapter Seven

"What's that you're reading?" Wendy asked Bridget on Monday as they settled at the group project table.

"Just a book on pagan holidays I picked up at the public library this weekend."

Dwayne glanced at it. "*Pagan* holidays?"

"Aye," Bridget answered. "Irish history goes back a long way."

"You better not let The Hound see it," Wendy said. "He'll probably think it's devil-worship or something."

Bridget's eyes widened. "But it's not. It's simply the way people worshipped before Christianity."

"That's true." Kevin grinned. "There's even a day named for you, I think."

Wendy noticed Bridget's blush as she looked down. Great. Just what she needed. Gallant knight Sir Kevin worshiping Bridget. She didn't want to ask, but she had to know. "What day is that?"

"Imbolc. February 1st. The Celts believed Brighid— spelled differently—was a fertility goddess who helped women with childbirth. When the priests came to Ireland, they changed the festival to a Christian one, calling it Candlemas and claiming *Saint* Brighid was the handmaid to the Virgin Mary."

"So Bridget is named after a saint?" Dwayne asked.

"I am nae a saint." Bridget's cheeks grew pinker. "Anyway, I remembered something about the Romans and the February celebration of Lupercalia from *Julius Caesar*, so that's what I was looking for. It's celebrated the same time as Valentine's."

Wendy didn't want to think about Valentine's…or the dance coming up. "The Romans ran through the streets to celebrate, didn't they?"

"Except Marc Antony refused, so the rest of the senators did too—"

"That's not the real meaning of Lupercal," Dwayne said. "If you actually do the research, you will find that the Romans sacrificed a goat and a dog, then used their skins to beat women."

Bridget gasped. "That sounds horrible!"

Dwayne raised one brow slightly. "The women actually lined up to get hit."

"Why would they do something awful like that?" Wendy tried to keep her voice from shaking.

"Because the dog represented purification and the goat fertility, so it was kind of like good luck." Dwayne smirked. "So maybe the story of your goddess isn't so far off."

Kevin scowled. "Don't compare Brighid to that…that bloody story."

Wendy wasn't sure if Kevin meant the Celtic goddess or the person sitting here at the table, but she didn't miss the grateful smile Bridget-in-the-flesh gave Kevin. Worse, he smiled back.

Dwayne shrugged. "It's true. Don't blame me."

"Let's change the subject." Kevin leveled a steady gaze on Dwayne. "This has nothing to do with our project."

"It might." Dwayne shrugged again. "One of the topics is counter-culture, and Neo-paganism is part of the

New Age thing, isn't it?"

"It's not part of *our* project," Kevin replied. "So let's move on."

"Yes! Let's," Bridget said. "Valentine's is supposed to be about romance and candy and cute cards."

Kevin smiled. "I totally agree."

Wendy frowned and pulled out her notes, not looking at Kevin. What had he actually agreed to?

****

By the time Kevin reached Government class on Wednesday afternoon, the news that the *USS Pueblo* had been attacked by North Korea the day before had already spread through the school. As disturbing as the incident was, he hoped it would at least unify the class.

And maybe eliminate the rift he'd started to sense with Wendy. She'd hardly said more than "hi" the past two days.

He pushed that thought aside as he took his seat. Apart from the disgusting conversation they'd had at their table on Monday, friction with their group projects had begun to divide the students as well. He could feel the hostility amongst some of them. In Tim's group, a guy named Mark who always wore a headband and favored tie-dyed shirts argued there was nothing wrong with dodging the draft. Tim, somewhat to Kevin's surprise, had argued equally loudly that every able-bodied male had a duty to his country. But then, the twins' father was career military, so maybe it did make sense.

In Tommy's group, Lionel was turning out to be quite vocal about Civil Rights, siding more with the Black Panthers approach than Martin Luther King's.

And, in Kevin's own group, Dwayne was blaming

the government for making LSD illegal, insisting the psychological experiments Timothy Leary conducted at Harvard proved it was beneficial.

That stance didn't endear their group to Mr. Kyle, and Bridget had voiced concerns about their grade.

Wendy hadn't been quick to agree.

Although Kevin seriously doubted she actually approved of the drug—or any others—she had taken to listening to Dwayne, even when he seemed to be ranting, and asking him lots of questions. He'd gone from being totally withdrawn to nearly pontificating, at least on his chosen subject. And Wendy acted like they should actually take the guy's opinion seriously.

But that wasn't the root of Kevin's problem with her. He wasn't sure what was.

"All right, class," Mr. Kyle said, "I'm suspending today's lesson so we can discuss what happened with our ship. Opinions?"

"North Korea accused us of being in their waters." Mark shrugged. "We didn't have any business being there anyway."

"We were monitoring Russian naval activity," Tim returned hotly.

"Yeah, do you want the Commies to come here?" Tommy demanded.

Mark shrugged again. "Is it fair that in America the rich get richer?"

"I heard a sailor was killed," Bridget said.

"Was he black?" Lionel asked.

She gave him a quizzical look. "What difference does that make?"

"Plenty, if you're black," Lionel replied. "Black kids get drafted more often than white kids do."

Mark nodded. "Because the rich white kids get deferments."

Lionel eyed him. "You're white, man."

"Yeah, but I'm not rich. I'm going to Canada as soon as I graduate."

Mr. Kyle intervened. "That's not the point of this discussion. The crew was taken prisoner and, if the reports are accurate, bound, beaten and tortured. Let's discuss human rights."

"Don't forget human rights are black rights," Lionel said.

"And brown and yellow and red too." Tim glared at him. "Don't make everything about you."

Lionel glared back. "Someone has to stand up for us."

"Everyone gets treated the same under Communism," Mark said.

"*Gentlemen.*" Although the word was polite, Mr. Kyle's tone gave no quarter for more argument. "Human rights are everyone's rights. What we should be discussing is military aggression by a country that we are not engaged with in war."

"Actually, we are," Dwayne said in a bored tone. "Victory was never declared, only an Armistice that led to a cease-fire, but no peace treaty."

"That is technically correct," Mr. Kyle answered.

Wendy smiled at Dwayne. "You are so smart."

He looked at her briefly and gave a curt nod that to Kevin looked conceited as all-get-out. As the class began to argue the points of what being at war actually meant and who was involved and what rights should prisoners-of-war have, he lost interest in the discussion. Not that it wasn't important, but what kept recycling in his mind was why Wendy kept being so nice to a guy who acted like he was doing them all a favor by being in the room.

Kevin doubted he'd ever understand girls.

****

Winter returned with a vengeance in February. Temperatures dropped to sub-zero and blizzards actually caused school to close several times, which was nearly unheard of in Minnesota. Drifts piled to seven or eight feet in places.

"If the snow keeps falling, we aren't going to dig our way out until after Easter," Wendy grumbled as she and Jo kept their mittened hands on the tether between the farmhouse and the barn. "I can hardly see you and you're right in front of me."

"And I feel like I'm walking in a swirling cloud of white nothingness," Jo answered, her voice muffled by the wool scarf across her face. "At least the horses are safe."

After what seemed an eternity trekking across the yard, they finally reached the barn door. Jo opened and then quickly shut it once they were inside.

The aroma of sweet hay permeated the air, while the heat from the animals hit Wendy's face like an opened oven. She unwrapped her scarf and drew off her mittens while the three horses stuck curious heads over the half-doors of their stalls.

Jo pulled out apple slices. "I hope these didn't freeze while we were out there."

"I don't think it matters to them," Wendy said, taking several for Jupiter.

"Probably not." Jo fed slices to Flame and Silver, who were both pushing their muzzles against her hands for more. "Okay, you guys have to take turns."

In response, Silver lifted both front hooves to stomp the ground and Flame pawed the door. Jupiter, hearing the commotion, added a whinny.

"I think they're bored," Jo said.

"Silver is going to be a real handful if you can't exercise him soon," Wendy replied.

"I know." Jo stroked his silken neck to calm him. "It's a good thing we got that ride in to the old bridge a couple of weeks ago."

The ride had ended in disappointment, at least for Wendy. Kevin had spent most of the road back talking to Jo about Luke's tracking skills, which he seemed fascinated about. Jo had been happy to chatter on—as she always did when the subject was Luke—and suggested Kevin spend some time with him over spring break.

Wendy wasn't sure whether Kevin had kept the conversation on Luke to keep Jo's mind off her cave experience or whether he wanted to keep the topic off Bridget. Either way, he'd left them at the fork in the road and they'd returned home without him.

Jo glanced over at her as she broke open a hay bale to feed the horses. "I know that ride didn't go like you wanted."

Wendy kept her eyes averted as she pulled out a bunch of hay for Jupiter. Sometimes, it seemed that Jo had the uncanny ability to read minds. "It went okay. The horses got some exercise."

"That's not what I meant," Jo answered. "You and Kevin didn't really get a chance to talk."

"Sure we did. We talked about diversity." Maybe she could divert Jo to another subject. "It seems like things are really changing at our high school. Mayberry

RFD may be disappearing."

Jo, however, was like a terrier with a bone. "That's not the point either. Last year, you and Kevin joked around with each other. This year, you're as stiff and formal as though you really were in King Arthur's court."

Wendy tried one more distraction. "Going to the old broken bridge was hardly the road to Camelot."

Jo was not to be deterred. "What gives with you two?"

"Nothing."

"Humph. You know what I think?" Jo went on before Wendy could say she didn't. "I think you both are too scared to be the first one to admit you really like each other a lot."

"Don't be silly." Wendy opened the stall door and busied herself with spreading the hay in Jupiter's manger, but when she emerged, Jo was grinning at her.

"What?"

"I'm right, aren't I?"

Wendy sighed. "I told you before. The guy is supposed to act first."

"Not if he thinks he's going to get rejected," Jo said. "Last year, you—"

"Things were different last year." When Jo just stood there, she added, "Besides, I don't want to get rejected either."

"Why do you think you will?"

Wendy rolled her eyes. "Have you forgotten Bridget? Kevin mentions her like every other sentence."

"He does not. They're both from Ireland, so why wouldn't they be friends?"

"Friends? How can a guy be friends with someone

who looks like Elizabeth Taylor, for Pete's sake?"

"She doesn't—"

"Yes, she does. Lots of guys think so." Wendy picked up a pail to get water. "Anyway, you can't deny Bridget is very pretty."

"You're cute too."

"I have *freckles*!"

Jo smiled. "Which some guys think are cute. Anyway, this isn't about looks. It's about you being scared to take a chance."

Wendy turned on the water tap. "I'm not *scared*."

"Then prove it," Jo answered. "Ask Kevin to the Sadie Hawkins Valentine's dance."

"I couldn't."

"Why not? Girls are *supposed* to ask boys for that. It's your perfect chance."

"But what if—"

"What if? What if he says 'yes'? What if he brings you a corsage and pins it on? What if you have a really wonderful time? *What if…*" Jo paused. "*What if* he kisses you?"

The thought of Kevin putting his arms around her and pulling her close, then dipping his head to press his mouth to hers made Wendy's knees feel like jelly while other parts of her tingled. What would his lips feel like? Would they be soft or firm? Would they be warm? Her own suddenly were. What if he slid his tongue…

"You might want to turn off the water," Jo said.

Her voice also turned off Wendy's suddenly rampant imagination. She looked down at the water sloshing over the bucket's rim and quickly reached for the spigot.

And prayed Jo couldn't read her mind about kissing

Kevin.

****

School was cancelled again on Monday and Tuesday, causing the weathermen on TV to keep exclaiming what a phenomenal start to the year it was. By the time they all got back to school on Wednesday, Wendy was heartily ready for spring thaws.

But first, there was the matter of Valentine's Day, which was only a week away. Since it fell on a Wednesday, the Sadie Hawkins dance wouldn't be until Friday, but time was running out.

She'd spent the past three days agonizing over what Jo had said. The "what if's" kept resounding in her head, especially the one possibility of Kevin kissing her. Valentine's wasn't like Christmas with its tradition of hanging mistletoe to accidently stand under, but it was Cupid's holiday—in spite of Dwayne's version—which was meant for couples to engage in romantic notions.

So, when she woke to the sun shining this morning, her spirits had risen too. Today was the day she was going to ask Kevin to go to the dance.

He wasn't on the bus this morning, which wasn't unusual since Mr. Lambart usually dropped him off on his way to work. She'd hoped to catch Kevin at lunch, but the twins were there. Now it was the last period of the day. Time really was running out.

"Since we didn't get to break into groups on Monday," Mr. Kyle said as the bell rang, "I've decided to let you work on your projects today,"

Chairs scraped noisily on the wood floor as students hurried to the tables in the back of the room. Wendy was pretty sure none of them were that eager to work, but everyone was probably stir-crazy from being snowed in for days. And, it would give her the opportunity to ask Kevin to stay a minute after the bell rang rather than to have to hurry out the door after him.

"I'm so glad to be back at school." Bridget took a seat. "I've missed you."

Since the phone lines had gone down with the blizzard, Wendy wondered if Bridget meant all of them or just Kevin. She'd taken a seat next to him. Wendy quickly sat down on his other side. It might look a little silly for all three of them to be piled together, since Dwayne was absent and the other side of the table was totally clear, but Wendy wasn't about to move there.

"I sure hope this snow melts fast and we can ride again," she said to Kevin. "The horses didn't get enough exercise last week."

"I know," Kevin answered. "I'm looking forward to the Hill Riders Club getting together again too."

Wendy nodded. "I really need to practice my roping to win at the horse show."

"Horse show? The Hill Riders Club?" Bridget asked.

"It's a club we started several years ago," Wendy said. "Lots of kids around here have horses and we thought we'd get together and organize an annual show."

"That sounds like fun!" Bridget exclaimed. "I loved riding in Ireland."

Wendy struggled to keep her face impassive. Just her luck that Bridget not only knew how to ride but loved it. On the bright side, though, the Hoffmans didn't have horses. "Well, we ride western and you were probably used to English saddle."

"That's true."

Kevin turned thoughtful. "Didn't Janie Nelsen ride

both English and western?"

Janie had been Billy Hoffman's steady girlfriend before he was killed last year. Wendy gave Kevin a wary look. "Yes. Why?"

"Mrs. Lambart said the Hoffmans told her Janie didn't come home from college for the holidays because the memories were still too bad. If her parents kept her horse, maybe they'd let Bridget ride it once the weather gets warm."

Bridget gave him a huge smile. "I'd *love* that!"

Kevin turned to Wendy. "Do you know if the Nelsens kept the horse?"

Wendy forced a smile of her own. It certainly seemed luck wasn't on her side today. "I'm not sure."

Bridget nearly bounced in her seat. "I'll ask Mrs. Hoffman about it tonight."

Mr. Kyle frowned at them, which thankfully brought the conversation to a close. Wendy tried not to feel resentful. Her mother would scold her for not being more charitable. Jo would probably tell her it was just one more reason she should make the first move and ask Kevin to the dance. Once she'd established that she had an actual date with Kevin, things would work themselves out.

They spent the rest of the period reviewing notes, and by the time the bell rang, Wendy was feeling better. Just a few more minutes…

She gave Bridget time to stand and gather her books. Then she turned to Kevin. "Could I talk to you for a minute?"

He put his books back on the table. "Sure."

"I want to wait until the twins leave," she said, hoping Bridget would take the hint.

She nearly groaned when the twins chose that moment to come over and engage Bridget in conversation. Then her mouth nearly fell open when they maneuvered her between them and walked out. Good gosh. Did the twins suspect what she wanted to do? Or worse, had Jo *told* them? They weren't usually this helpful. Were they up to something?

"What did you want to talk about?" Kevin broke into her thoughts.

"Oh...ah..." Wendy tried to calm what felt like a couple of dozen butterflies taking flight in her stomach. "I was just wondering..."

"Aye?"

"Ah...that is... Well, would you go to the Sadie Hawkins dance with me?"

There. She'd said it. The butterflies calmed, then suddenly took flight again as she realized he wasn't answering. Instead, he had the strangest look on his face.

Finally, he spoke. "Bridget has already asked me—"

"Oh! Forget I said anything then!" Face flaming, Wendy bolted past him and out the door.

"Wait!" he called after her.

She didn't stop. She was going to die of mortification. Tim and Tommy probably *knew* Kevin already had a date which was why they were pretending to be helpful. How was she going to face their teasing? And Jo...her cousin was going to get an earful, too. She should never have pushed Wendy to ask Kevin for a date.

But first, she was going to have to get home. There was no way she was going to get on the school bus with all of them. No way.

She started walking and then broke into a run.

Chapter Eight

Kevin rushed out the door and down the hall, nearly colliding with The Hound, who bellowed for him to slow down, but he was already out the door. He ran past a startled Bridget waiting by the entrance and raced to the bus just as the door was closing. He pulled it open, causing the bus driver to frown at him. Before he could step in, though, he spotted a figure running in the distance, wearing a red sweater. That had to be Wendy.

"Never mind," he said to the driver as he spun around to follow her.

He slipped and slid on the icy sidewalk and wished he'd worn sneakers instead of hard-heeled boots. Ahead of him, Wendy must have been having the same problems, because she veered off into the banked snow which, thanks to its depth, slowed her progress considerably. He stuck to the sidewalk, his arms waving like a pinwheel to help keep his balance. Even so, he caught himself stumbling forward a couple of times, probably looking like one of his uncles who'd spent a little too much time in the pub. At the moment, though, he didn't much care how he looked.

"Wendy! Wait up! *Cá bhfuil tú ag dul?*"

Glancing over her shoulder at the sound of his voice just seemed to spur her on. She broke into an awkward run, this time hopping over piled snow much like a filly learning to jump hurdles. If he hadn't been so intent on catching her—and avoiding sprawling flat himself—he'd have admired how her jean-clad legs seemed to split in the air as she cleared low drifts.

He plunged through the snow, his task a bit easier now since Wendy had left more or less of a path. "Wait!" he called again, wondering if he should save his energy.

Wendy slowed. He wasn't sure it was because he was closer or whether she was as out-of-breath as he was. He doubled his efforts and managed to grasp her arm.

"Whoa, lass!"

She turned on him furiously. "I'm not a horse, Kevin O'Keefe."

"Aye. I mean, nae, ye aren't. I just wanted ye to stop." Kevin looked closer. "Are ye cryin'?"

Wendy swiped at her nose with an ungloved hand. "I am *not* crying."

He squinted. "Then why is your face wet?"

She glared at him. "It's cold out here. My eyes watered."

"But…" Kevin closed his mouth abruptly. His sister, Mary, hated to be caught crying. Better to change the subject. "Why did ye run away?"

She pulled at the sleeves of her sweater, bunching her hands under the cuffs, and didn't answer.

Kevin pulled off his jacket. "Here. Put this on."

Wendy shook her head. "You'll freeze."

"Ye left yer coat in the room, so ye'll freeze if ye don't take it.." He stepped forward to wrap it around her shoulders. For one brief moment, he held her in a near embrace, catching the subtle scent of the shampoo she used. His hands brushed the sides of her neck as he pulled the jacket close around her and heard her quick little gasp. He paused for a second, tempted to stroke that soft skin once more. Then he dropped his hands and stepped back.

"Ye have nae told me why ye ran."

She looked down. "I was embarrassed when you turned me down."

"But I did nae turn ye down."

Wendy raised her eyes. "You told me Bridget asked you first."

"Aye, she did. But 'tis a Sadie Hawkins dance, nae?" When Wendy nodded, he went on. "Then that means more than one girl can ask. I will be happy to escort both of ye."

Wendy stared at him for so long that he wondered if she'd answer. One of the guys in his shop class had explained this was a very casual dance, not anything like prom, and another guy had agreed. Kevin personally thought his was a brilliant idea. Bridget was definitely homesick and needed a friend. Escorting Wendy would be one step closer to actually asking *her* for a real date.

"Lass? What do ye think?"

She began to sputter. "I… I think…you…"

They were interrupted by the sound of a car coming to a stop just behind them. Kevin turned around to see Mr. Hoffman at the wheel.

"Bridget said she saw the two of you running this way." He gestured to the back seat. "Hop in before you freeze to death."

Since he was trying to keep his teeth from chattering, Kevin wasn't about to argue the point, although Wendy looked like she wanted to.

"Ye can't walk five miles in this cold, even with my jacket," he said and grasped her arm lightly, just in case she decided to bolt again. "Come on. The car's warm."

Although she still looked mutinous, she must have realized the wisdom of his words, since she sighed and then nodded.

Once they were settled inside the car, Bridget turned in the front seat to give them a puzzled look.

"What were ye two doin' out here in the cold?" She looked at Kevin's jacket around Wendy's shoulders and frowned. "What are ye doin' without your own coat?"

Wendy gave him a sideways glance. "Kevin can explain better than I can."

Kevin suddenly sensed that, with both girls watching him, his plan might not be all that brilliant after all.

"'Tis a long story, best left for tellin' another time."

Wendy raised an eyebrow and Bridget frowned again. Kevin caught Mr. Hoffman watching him in the rearview mirror with what seemed to be a sympathetic look, although maybe he was just imagining that.

"The boy's near frozen. Let him thaw out," Mr. Hoffman said. "You girls can talk later."

Kevin breathed a sigh of relief. A reprieve. At least for a little while.

****

"I can't believe Kevin actually expects me to be his second date," Wendy complained to Jo after they'd both gotten home and were now settled on their twin beds drinking hot cocoa. "Who does he think he is?"

Jo licked some of the marshmallow foam off her chocolate. "Is it really such a bad idea?"

"*What*?"

"Would you rather he escort just Bridget?"

"*No*." The idea of Kevin on a date with Bridget made her hand shake and she almost spilled her drink.

"He didn't have to say yes to her."

Jo raised a brow. "Why wouldn't he? *You* hadn't asked him."

Wendy lifted her chin. "I was going to."

"You dawdled. Admit it."

"You don't have to be so blasted practical." She glared at her cousin. Jo knew how she felt about making the first move.

"I'm not trying to make you mad," Jo replied, "but I do think if you'd asked earlier, he wouldn't have made the same offer to take Bridget along."

"I'm not too sure about that." Wendy put her cup down on the small table and flopped back on her bed to stare at the ceiling. "She sticks to him like a cocklebur and he doesn't seem to mind."

"I think he's just being nice to her." Jo set her mug down too. "He's always acted like a gentleman."

Wendy couldn't deny that. He'd taken off his jacket in freezing weather and given it to her since she'd run out of school like an idiot without hers. She could still feel its warmth along with the slight scent he always wore. Or maybe that had come directly from him. He'd stood awfully close as he draped the jacket over her. Remembering how his fingers had brushed the bare skin of her neck sent tingles down her spine and she smiled in spite of herself.

"What are you grinning about?" Jo asked.

"Nothing." Wendy sat up and reached for her chocolate.

Jo eyed her for a moment. "So…what did you tell him?"

"I didn't. Mr. Hoffman picked us up before I could answer, and he dropped Kevin off first." Wendy grimaced. "Bridget was in the car too."

"Well, she is living with the Hoffmans," Jo pointed out. "But remember, she didn't know anything about Kevin's offer to take both of you to the dance. She might not like it either."

"That's too bad," Wendy retorted. "Kevin asked me to go with them."

Jo smiled. "Then I take it you're going to say yes?"

"I… I…" Wendy hesitated and then sighed. "What choice do I have?"

"You could let Bridget go alone with him."

"*That* is *not* an option."

Jo's smile widened. "I didn't think it would be."

Wendy frowned. Somehow she got the feeling that she'd just been out-maneuvered. It looked like she'd have to swallow her pride after all, unless she wanted to sit home and brood while Kevin danced with Bridget at the Sadie Hawkins.

That was *definitely* not an option.

****

The twins were waiting at the lunch table the next day when Wendy set her tray down. She had dreaded this moment ever since she got to school this morning. Word had spread about her mad dash outside without a coat yesterday and Kevin chasing after her. She'd managed to persuade her mother to drive Jo and herself to school rather than ride the bus, and she'd lingered at the house so long that they'd almost been tardy, but at least she hadn't had to face any kids or questions.

Until now. Tommy and Tim looked at her expectantly, for once both quiet.

"It's supposed to warm up this weekend. Maybe we can get the horses out again." Wendy hoped the topic would distract the twins.

It didn't. They both just stared.

Jo unwrapped her sandwich. "You might as well just tell them."

Wendy pushed some of the macaroni-hamburger casserole they all just called "hot dish" around on her plate with her fork. "Tell them what?"

"You might start with why you decided to run out of school like the building was on fire yesterday," Tommy said. "Without your coat, like it was summer."

"And why was Kevin chasing after you, yelling like some medieval warrior?" Tim asked.

"I guess he wanted to know where I was going."

"Stop playing stupid, cousin," Tommy said.

"Yeah, answer the question," Tim added. "Why were you both out there?"

Wendy glared at both of them. "Like you two don't really know."

Tommy turned to Jo. "Did her brain freeze while she was out there? Why would we ask if we already knew why she was acting crazy?"

Tim grinned. "Craz-*ier*, you mean."

"Oh, stop it! Both of you." Wendy tossed her fork down, sloshing some hot dish over the edge of her tray. "Like you didn't lead Bridget away yesterday so I could make a fool of myself."

Both of the twins blinked, then looked at each other.

"She *is* crazy," Tommy said.

Tim frowned. "We were only giving you a chance to ask Kevin to the dance."

"Like you didn't know Bridget had already asked him!"

"We *didn't*," they said in unison.

"Geez, if we'd known—"

"Yeah, we're sorry."

Wendy gave them both wary looks. They seemed sincere, but she'd known them all their lives. "Do you swear?"

"We swear," they answered together.

Then Tommy added, "Are you still planning to still go?"

"Maybe you should ask Dwayne and make Kevin jealous," Tim suggested.

"That's silly," Jo said, "and totally unnecessary."

"It is?"

"Yes." Jo glanced at Wendy. "Tell them the rest."

For a moment, Wendy wanted to throttle Jo, then she sighed. Kevin had called last night and they'd talked. Everyone would find out soon enough anyway, so she might as well get it over with.

"As it turns out, Kevin will be taking both Bridget and me to the dance," she said.

The twins looked at each other again and then they both burst out laughing. Practically howling. Wendy drew her brows together. "What's so funny?"

The bell rang, ending the lunch period. Tommy just shook his head as they got up, but Tim managed to speak between chortles. "We didn't know Kevin was such a glutton for punishment." Then the twins walked away, still chuckling.

****

Surprisingly, Tim and Tommy didn't broadcast Wendy's having to share Kevin with Bridget for the Sadie Hawkins dance, and by the weekend, gossip had ceased about Wendy's wild dash into the snow, although she still got a few curious looks.

And, surprisingly too, Bridget didn't seem to be upset over the arrangements for the dance either. Not that they really talked about it. Kevin had suggested they'd surprise everyone instead. They just shrugged if anyone asked if any of them had a date.

Still, by the time Friday evening arrived, Wendy was far more nervous than she thought she would be. Her stomach felt like a bevy of quails kept getting startled.

"I wish you were coming to the dance, Jo."

Her cousin smiled. "I wouldn't have much to do without Luke there."

"You could still get out on the floor. Not everything is going to be slow-dancing." At least, she didn't think it would. The Hound didn't approve of PDAs—public displays of affection—so usually the only slow dance was the last one and maybe one halfway through.

The stomach birds took flight again. Who would Kevin choose for the last dance? Maybe, if there was a slow dance in the middle, she should encourage Bridget to take it, even though she didn't want to see them dancing together. Still, it would mean the last dance would be *her* turn. Wouldn't it? She couldn't bear it if she had to sit out the last dance—a *slow* dance—like a wallflower.

This night was going to turn out awful.

"Stop it," Jo said.

Wendy gave her a startled look. She didn't think she'd spoken out loud. Had she? "What?"

"Whatever you're thinking," Jo answered. "You look like you're going to be sick."

That was more accurate than her cousin knew. "I really don't know if it was so smart of me to accept. No other guy is going to have two dates."

Jo raised an eyebrow. "Just think how much more miserable you would be sitting home tonight."

"You're sitting home."

"That's different and you know it. Besides, since Kevin doesn't have an American driver's license yet, Mrs. Lambart will be bringing all three of you home. It's not like there's going to be any hanky-panky going on with Bridget."

Or with her either. She had her license and her original idea had been to offer to drive, since that meant she could drop Bridget off first and be alone with Kevin. Unfortunately, her mother had vetoed that idea.

"Just don't worry about everything," Jo said. "Think about just having fun."

Wendy supposed Jo was right when, a half hour later, her mother dropped her off in front of the school gym. Kevin was waiting at the door and smiled as she approached.

"I have somethin' for ye," he said after they'd gotten inside as far as the foyer and she tossed her coat on a pile with others by the door. He opened a small box he'd been holding and lifted out a wrist corsage of red and white carnations. "I ken the dance is casual, but I thought ye'd like this anyway."

"I do!" Wendy held out her hand for him to fasten it, liking the feel of his fingers caressing her wrist as he did. Was it deliberate? She noticed he didn't have *two* boxes.

"Shall we go in?"

As they stepped through the second set of doors to the gym, Wendy took a moment to appreciate the decorating effort. In one corner, snacks and a punch bowl sat on a white butcher-paper covered table with red hearts pasted all over it. In the opposite corner, a DJ had set up a strobe light over his stand. Although not as elaborate as prom would be, red and white crepe paper streamers extended from the gym's center hanging light to the basketball hoops at either end and to the tops of the pushed-back bleachers on either side. With the strobe and only half the gym lights on, the effect was a flashing, peppermint-like canopy that felt romantic. If she could just have the last dance...

"Does it nae look nice?"

Wendy turned to see that Bridget stood behind her. From where she stood, Wendy couldn't see if she had a corsage or not. "Have you been here long?"

Bridget shook her head. "Just a few minutes before you, but I didn't want to stand out in the cold."

At least, Kevin hadn't offered Bridget his coat while he waited. Then that smug thought was flattened when Bridget raised her hand and Wendy saw she wore a corsage too. She should have known Kevin would buy one for each of them. She could almost hear Jo saying as much.

The music started with a booming version of "Kicks" and Kevin gestured toward the open floor. "Shall we?"

Did he mean both of them? Wendy glanced around. A number of kids had come without dates and were bunched together, already hopping around.

"Sure." As they joined the others, no one seemed to take much notice that Kevin was here with two girls. The twins, thankfully, were concentrating on their steady dates, and Wendy began to relax as the evening wore on. Kevin wasn't only an agile dancer but managed to spin Bridget and her without their bumping into each other.

She even noticed a few of the guys who'd come stag were asking two girls to dance at once, although some of the resulting moves looked pretty pathetic compared to Kevin.

When the lights blinked, signaling an intermission for the DJ and the first notes of "Groovin'" started playing, Kevin hesitated. Wendy felt courageous enough to suggest he dance with Bridget, if she could claim the next slow dance.

He looked surprised, but readily agreed. She pushed aside the niggling guilt that neither Bridget nor Kevin knew it would be the *last* dance and almost always "Blue Velvet." She loved that song.

Since she didn't want to watch them dance and she didn't want to stand by the punch bowl alone, Wendy decided she'd get some fresh air. The gym had grown stuffy.

Pawing her way through the pile of coats, she found hers and slipped it on, then stepped outside. And nearly ran into Dwayne. She jumped, startled.

"I didn't see you inside."

"I didn't go in."

Wendy frowned. "Why not? Lots of kids came alone."

"I didn't feel like it." Dwayne looked over her shoulder to the door she'd left ajar. "Are you and Bridget both dating O'Keefe?"

"I…no." Wendy wondered how he'd known they were together since he hadn't come in. "We…just came together."

He gave her a long look. "Interesting."

She wasn't sure what he meant by that either, but she turned to go. "You're welcome to come in."

A corner of his mouth lifted slightly. "Not tonight."

"Okay, then." Wendy felt him watching her as she went back in, but she didn't turn around. He certainly could act strangely.

The music hadn't started up when she joined Kevin and Bridget, who were standing off to one side. The lights had been turned all the way up and the Hound stood by the punch bowl, glaring at everyone.

"What's going on?" she asked.

"Someone put a wee drop of whiskey in the punch," Kevin said.

Bridget giggled. "I think it was more than a wee drop."

"Aye, I suspect ye are right."

Wendy widened her eyes. "And the Hound found out?"

"Aye. He took a glass."

Wendy groaned. "Oh, no. Who would be stupid enough to do this?"

"'Tis what Mr. Hund was askin' as ye came in."

Wendy scoured the room for Tim and Tommy. It sounded like some kind of prank they would pull, but if the twins had anything to do with this, they were going to be in serious trouble. No alcohol was ever allowed. Even their father wouldn't be able to keep them from getting expelled.

She finally spotted them across the gym with Susan and Carla. They didn't look particularly guilty, but they'd had years to perfect their expressions. Catching Tommy's eye, she narrowed hers. He'd understand the silent question.

Shaking his head, he crossed his heart and Wendy breathed a sigh of relief. That was the one gesture she knew he wouldn't use if he were hiding anything, since his dad had emphasized it was akin to being a traitor if he used it to lie. She turned her attention back to The Hound, who was still glaring.

"Unless someone owns up to this prank *now*," he said, "the dance is over."

When silence greeted him, Wendy groaned again. If the assistant principal couldn't find the culprit, they'd be lucky to have a prom this spring.

"That's it, then," he said. "Everyone go home."

Wendy cast another look in the twins' direction. *Tim* had better not have had anything to do with this.

It had just cost her the last dance of the evening with Kevin.

Chapter Nine

But the following Monday morning, the mystery of who'd spiked the punch took a back seat to the news that a Vietnam general had shot a Viet Cong officer openly on a Saigon street. The incident had actually occurred on the first of February but had been kept under wraps.

"I don't know what everyone is so upset about," Dwayne said during Government class. "It wasn't even anyone in the U.S. Army that did it."

"But the man—Bay Lop—was murdered in cold blood," Bridget responded. "He had already been arrested."

"Isn't that why LBJ keeps sending our guys over there?" Mark asked. "To kill off the Viet Cong?"

"We're not over there just to kill people," Tommy said. "We're trying to keep the South Vietnamese free from Communism."

"People still get killed, don't they?" Mark looked disgruntled. "The Vietnamese would probably rather live as Communists than be dead."

"Our dad says Communism is oppressive and makes people government slaves," Tim said.

"How is that different from the way the draft over here works?" Mark raised a brow. "Unless guys are smart enough—or rich enough—to get into college, they don't have a choice when their number comes up."

"Tell me about it," Lionel said. "Black folks get

called up way more often than white folks do."

Dwayne gave him a level look. "Why is that, do you suppose?"

Lionel stared back. "Most black folks don't have rich daddies to get them deferments or the money to go to college—in Detroit, anyway."

"You can get a scholarship…if you're smart."

"Dwayne's right," Wendy said. "Everyone who wants to go to college should apply for scholarships. I did."

Dwayne gave her a small smile. "You're smart enough to get in."

"Are you saying I'm not?" Lionel started to rise.

"I think colleges base acceptance on lots of things," Kevin said quickly. "I know at Notre Dame the grades are only one part of it."

"Kevin is correct." Mr. Kyle moved between Lionel and Dwayne. "But the class discussion is not on college requirements. We were talking about unnecessary violence."

"When is violence ever necessary?" Mark asked.

"Good point." The teacher studied him, then looked at the rest of the class. "Opinions?"

Several hands rose at once and Wendy leaned back in her chair. They'd almost had a violent incident right here in class. Fights in class had never happened in Middletown before.

****

"Why did you agree that Dwayne was right?" Tim asked Wendy after school as they waited for the school bus.

"About scholarships?" Wendy blinked. "Anyone can apply."

"That wasn't what Dwayne meant," Tommy said. "He was trying to start something with Lionel."

"Why would he do that?"

"I don't know," Tommy answered. "Maybe he's prejudiced."

"Because Lionel is black?" Jo asked.

Tommy shrugged. "Discrimination is happening all over the country. Why can't it happen here?"

"We've never had *any* minorities move in," Tim added. "The Jacksons are the first ones."

"So?" Wendy frowned at him. "We should just accept Lionel for who he is."

"I'm not disagreeing with you, cousin. But practically every day, when we turn on the news there's something about a riot or a civil rights protest going on somewhere."

"And Dwayne is from Minneapolis, don't forget," Tommy said. "They have all kinds of minorities in the Twin Cities."

Tim nodded. "Not to mention Dwayne is a bit odd himself."

Wendy really couldn't argue that point, since his behavior outside the gym Friday night had certainly been weird. She'd practically forgotten about it, though, after The Hound had found the punch spiked and cancelled the rest of the dance. "Dwayne may act a little different because he feels he doesn't fit in either."

"Is that why you're so nice to him?" Tim asked.

"Sort of, I guess," Wendy answered. "When he got here he was so quiet and stuck to himself. Mrs. Lambart mentioned at our dinner that he might be shy."

Tommy snorted. "Shy, my foot."

"He probably thinks he's too good for us country

bumpkins," Tim said.

"He *does* act a little bit conceited," Jo agreed, "but I only have English class with him and he always knows all the answers, so maybe he's just smart."

"He *is* smart," Wendy said. "I think he likes it when I point that out."

Tommy gave her a contemplative look. "That sounds like you're buttering him up."

Wendy shook her head. "I just think giving a person compliments is good."

"Yeah." Tim grinned. "And maybe you're trying to make Kevin jealous?"

She glared at him. "I am *not*!"

"Hey!" He held up his hand. "It might work."

"I'm *not* going to play games."

"Well…" Tommy shrugged. "If you don't mind going on three-way dates—"

"Stop it!" Wendy felt herself blush. "You know darn well I had no control over how that came about."

"How what came about?" Kevin asked as he joined the group.

Wendy was sure her face was on fire as she dug through her book bag, pretending to look for something so she wouldn't have to answer. She only prayed Kevin had been too far away to hear any of the conversation.

"We were talking about the dance," Jo said smoothly. "What a pity it had to end so soon before you and Wendy could slow dance."

Wendy fervently wished an earthquake would suddenly create a big crack in the sidewalk and she could fall through. She dug deeper into her bag, not looking up.

"Aye, well." Kevin stooped low so he could speak directly to Wendy. "But there'll be another dance, won't there?"

"Ah…sure!" She straightened. If her face hadn't already been flaming from embarrassment, it certainly would be from bending over to try to bury herself in her bag. "I…hope so."

"Me too," Kevin said as the bus rolled up and he stepped aside to let her get on.

Thankfully, she climbed on, but she wasn't sure if she wanted to throttle Jo for what she'd said or to hug her.

****

Wendy looked for Kevin several days later as she entered Government class, but he wasn't there. She sighed. Tuesday, the day after the unfortunate—or fortunate—incident by the bus stop, Kevin had gone on a field trip with the Ag class to a breeding farm near Brainerd. On the way back, the bus had broken down in the middle of a snowstorm, causing them not only to get soaked and nearly freeze to death, but they'd had to stay overnight in St. Cloud. By the time they returned on Wednesday, the twins said Kevin had taken a fever and was hacking something terrible.

He hadn't yet returned to school. Wendy sighed. The snowstorm had also taken the telephone lines down across most of the state, so she'd hadn't even been able to call the Lambarts and ask about him.

Mr. Kyle finished taking roll as Mark burst into the room, waving a copy of the *Miami Herald.*

"Did you hear the latest? The Florida teachers have gone on strike! I guess teachers can rebel too."

"They aren't *rebelling,*" Mr. Kyle replied.

"No? They're refusing to go to work and staging protests and carrying signs." Mark shrugged. "Sounds like they're no different from the anti-war protestors."

Mr. Kyle closed the book he'd started to open. "The difference is the cause, although I suppose you do have a point. The teachers are striking because education was underfunded in the state budget and they want better pay and working conditions."

"Hey," someone quipped from the back of the room, "maybe Minnesota teachers should go on strike too. Then we'd have more vacation."

"Like we wouldn't have to make it up," Wendy said.

"Good point, Miss Wade," the teacher said. "I'm sure none of you would want to cut your summer short."

"No way!" someone else said.

"The teachers in Minneapolis were talking strikes last year," Dwayne mentioned.

Another student gave him a wide-eyed look. "Really? We didn't hear about it."

"You probably wouldn't," Dwayne answered in a bored tone. "Middletown is pretty much out of the news loop."

"It's true nothing much ever happens here," Wendy said.

Mr. Kyle gave them an appraising look. "And that's exactly why we should appreciate living here. Small towns aren't subject to all the chaos and riots and violence that the big cities have."

"That's what my dad said when he moved us here from Detroit," Lionel said, "but don't fool yourselves. It's coming."

"That sounds so negative. Mayberry—I mean, Middletown—has always been quiet and peaceful," Wendy answered.

Lionel shrugged. "Just sayin'."

"I hope you're wrong," Tommy said, "but then, who would have thought teachers would go on strike?"

"Yeah, you guys are supposed to be, like, pillars of the community," Tim added.

"This may surprise you," Mr. Kyle answered, "but teachers are actually human."

"Yeah, like the song…" Dwayne smirked and finished in soto-voce, "Born to be Wild."

Wendy gave him a covert look, not quite sure how to take that statement. Sometimes she thought the twins were right. He was odd.

****

Kevin finished another coughing fit and reached for the glass of water by his bed. By the saints! He'd never felt so miserable in his life. He shivered, even though the room was warm and Mrs. Lambart had brought enough blankets to weigh down a horse.

"I don't like the sound of that." The elderly doctor who still made house calls put away his stethoscope. "It sounds like it's settling in his lungs."

Mrs. Lambart hovered at the end of the bed. "Pneumonia?"

"Not yet, I think, but it may turn into that." The doctor rose and picked up his bag. "I've given him a penicillin shot and I'll have some antibiotics sent over."

She looked about ready to weep. "I should have called you sooner, Dr. Knutson, but I thought Kevin had just taken a cold from getting wet Tuesday."

"Don't blame yourself," Kevin managed to rasp out. "I should have worn snow boots."

"You should be saving your energy by not talking," the doctor said. "And be sure you drink a full glass of water every hour."

Kevin tried not to wince at that idea, but Mrs. Lambart nodded. "I'll make sure he does. What about food?"

"If the young man is hungry, feed him."

She turned to Kevin. "That nice Irish girl brought a casserole over last night, but you were sleeping so I put it in the refrigerator."

In spite of the doctor's warning not to strain his voice, he asked, "What kind?"

"She called it colcannon and said her brothers always wanted it when they got sick."

Colcannon. For an instant, he was back in Ireland, the familiar smells of cooked cabbage and mashed potatoes mixed with shallots and butter haunting his stuffed nose. He remembered his grandmother making it, swearing *her* recipe came from the Middle Ages.

"That sounds good."

"I'll go heat some up right now." Mrs. Lambart bustled out of the room, followed by the doctor.

Kevin stared into space after they left. He wasn't surprised that Bridget had known to make the casserole. Most Irish girls learned how to cook at an early age and a lot of families still relied on home remedies. Colcannon was a staple for curing what ailed a person. He wondered if Wendy knew how to cook too.

Thinking of Wendy caused his thoughts to drift to the dance. He'd been disappointed when she had encouraged him to slow dance with Bridget just before intermission. He'd almost offered to escort her outside when she said she needed some fresh air, but he'd reminded himself that he wasn't going to follow her around like a puppy this year. Besides, even though he thought of Bridget as a homesick friend, it would have been an insult to leave her standing there.

Then there had been that moment before the bus came on Monday. He didn't know what the whole conversation had been about, but he distinctly got the impression that Wendy didn't want to look at him. She'd practically buried her face in her book bag. And even when he'd mentioned—in what he'd hoped was a casual voice—about there being another dance, she'd hesitated in answering.

Maybe she didn't want to dance slow with him. His chest clenched and it wasn't from his illness. Maybe she wasn't any more interested in him this year than she had been last year when she was mooning after James.

Another fit of coughing overtook him and he reached for the water again. By St. Patrick! He needed to be back at school to find out. Setting the glass on the table, he flopped back on the pillows. He had a feeling that wasn't going to happen anytime soon.

Chapter Ten

"I'm feeling really nervous," Wendy said as she turned her mother's car onto the Lambarts' yard road on Saturday.

"Why?" Jo asked. "We're just paying a sick call. Kevin's been absent from school for over a week."

"Yes, but..." She let her voice trail off. When the phone lines had gone back up last week she'd called, but Mrs. Lambart said the doctor said he shouldn't exert himself. Then she'd called this past Tuesday, only to be told he was sleeping and Mrs. Lambart didn't want to wake him. This morning she'd decided to just come over, unannounced. It had seemed a good idea at the time. Now she wasn't so sure.

"I don't know why you're worried," Jo said. "We might not be able to stay long, but Kevin will be glad to see you anyway."

Wendy parked the car. She just hoped he wasn't trying to avoid her. Mrs. Lambart must have mentioned she'd called twice. He could have returned her calls. They'd not had any more storms, and the phones were working. She knew that for a fact since she checked the line several times each evening. Her nervousness grew as she took the candy and cookies she'd bought for him out of the back seat.

"I guess it's now or never."

Jo rolled her eyes. "This is not a life-or-death

situation, you know."

Wendy frowned. "Pneumonia can be."

"I wasn't talking about Kevin. I meant *you*."

"Still…" She didn't finish her sentence as the front door open and Mrs. Lambart waved at them.

"Come in, girls. Kevin's in the living room."

"I'm glad to hear he's up and about," Jo said as they walked inside. "Is he feeling better, then?"

"He still tires easily," Mrs. Lambart replied, "but he's getting bored sitting around, so he'll be glad you came."

Not exactly the reason Wendy wanted to hear, but she wasn't going to quibble. Kevin looked up from the recliner he was lounging in as they entered the living room and Wendy stumbled to a standstill.

He was wearing dark blue pajamas with a blue-and-green-plaid cape-like thing loosely draped over them. She'd never actually seen a guy in pajamas before and it seemed, suddenly, very intimate. Then she realized that wasn't what had caused her to stop. It was his face.

He had *stubble* on his face. It was darker than his auburn hair, which, always a bit longish, now nearly touched his shoulders. It was tousled, the stubborn lock falling over his forehead, accentuating his penetrating golden eyes. The whole effect made parts of her tingle. He looked…more like a *man*.

Jo gave her a nudge. She broke from her reverie and moved forward to set the candy and cookies down on the coffee table. "I brought you something."

Kevin smiled, his teeth flashing white as he nodded.

"Are you feeling better?"

He nodded again.

"Laryngitis," Mrs. Lambart said as she entered the

room and gestured for them to sit. "He lost his voice nearly a week ago from all the coughing."

Wendy felt nearly hysterical with relief as she sank onto the sofa. So that was why he didn't return her calls. He couldn't *talk*.

"When will you be able to return to school?" she asked and then felt like a moron since he couldn't speak. "Sorry. Don't try to answer."

"Sometime next week," Mrs. Lambart answered for him. "He's chomping at the bit to get back, too."

"Speaking of bits," Jo said. "We're getting ready to start saddling up to ride again on Saturdays. Hopefully, you can join us in a week or two."

Kevin bobbed his head vigorously, causing the lock of hair to fall into his eyes. Wendy had the oddest urge to brush it aside for him, although he had already tossed his head to accomplish that. She was certainly having strange reactions to him this morning.

Jo gave her a contemplative look. "Why don't you explain about our horse show?"

Grateful to have something to focus on besides how appealing Kevin looked with that shadowy stubble, Wendy proceeded to explain that their rider's club liked to put on a summer exhibition horse show and invite other riding clubs. She was just about to launch into how many events there would be when there was a knock on the door.

"Ah, that must be Bridget," Mrs. Lambart said as she rose. "She's been bringing over the most delicious Irish dishes. I swear, they've speeded up Kevin's recovery."

Wendy suddenly felt like one of her horse's hooves had kicked her in the stomach. Bridget had been coming over? On what sounded like a regular basis? And bringing home-cooked recipes from Ireland? She looked at her store-bought cookies on the table.

Kevin frowned slightly and shook his head. She wished she knew how to interpret that. He was giving her such an intense look that she nearly squirmed. Instead, she pasted a smile on her face. "I guess I don't need to fill you in on what's been happening at school then." No doubt Bridget had taken care of that.

"I'll just put this in the oven so it will stay warm," Wendy heard Bridget say from the hallway and Mrs. Lambart's response. Then the voices faded away.

Evidently, she knew her way around the house, too. The other hoof hit. Tears threatened to erupt and she stood quickly, practically pulling Jo up with her. "Well, we need to get going."

Kevin shook his head and gestured for them to sit.

"No, really." She had to get out of here before the tears poured out. She moved to the door. "We just stopped by to say hi. See you at school."

There was a croaking sound from Kevin, but she didn't turn around. Then she nearly collided with Mrs. Lambart and Bridget in the hall. Could her luck get any worse?

"Why are you leaving?" Mrs. Lambart asked. "You girls could have a nice visit."

Just what she didn't want to do.

"You could stay for lunch," Bridget said. "I made plenty."

That was even worse. Whatever Bridget had made smelled delicious, blast it. Wendy wouldn't be able to swallow a mouthful, though.

"We weren't planning to stay," she said. "My mom

needs the car back."

"Oh. Well, all right, then," Mrs. Lambart replied. "Say hello to Vivian for me."

Wendy nodded, not trusting her own voice any longer and nearly yanked Jo through the door with her.

Once outside, Jo pulled her arm away. "We really should have stayed for lunch, you know. That would have been the best strategy."

"You don't have to tell me. Here." She handed the keys to Jo and ran to the car as the tears began to flow.

****

Mo chreach-sa thàinig! Kevin tried to vocalize the sentiment as he stared after Wendy, but only another frog-like croak emerged. Of all the rotten timing. He was *Irish* and supposed to be *lucky*. Unless, of course, the faeries had deserted him because he liked America. Which might very well be the case, since he'd come down with this damnable illness. In Ireland, he never even caught a cold.

"I hope ye're hungry." Bridget came into the room with Mrs. Lambart. "I made haggerty since Mrs. Lambart said you really like bacon."

Kevin forced a smile to accompany his nod. He did have a particular liking for American bacon, with its thin, crispy slices. Bacon in Ireland was what would be called ham here. He just wished the dish hadn't arrived while Wendy was visiting.

At least she had come. He'd nearly been fit to be tied—except he didn't have the energy—when he learned that he had missed her calls. Two of them. And, since he couldn't speak, he couldn't call back. Had she thought him rude? Or worse, that he didn't care? He'd wanted to explain to her. He could have gotten a notebook and pen, but she'd left too abruptly once Bridget got here.

"Bridget has been giving me recipes for all sorts of Irish dishes." Mrs. Lambart beamed at her. "My husband can't decide if he likes the steak and mushroom pie best or the corned beef and cabbage."

"'Tis simple Irish fare," Bridget said, "although at home a wee bit of whiskey or ale might be added."

Mrs. Lambart's eyes twinkled. "I'll remember that."

"The Hoffmans like my breakfast porridge. I put cinnamon and brown sugar in it," Bridget said. "I could bring some over one mornin'."

"That would be delightful," Mrs. Lambart replied. "It certainly sounds better than our plain oatmeal."

Kevin shifted uncomfortably in his chair. He was glad Bridget got on so well with Mrs. Lambart. Bridget had told him the Hoffmans weren't given to much conversation… Mrs. Hoffman would lapse into silence after dinner and Mr. Hoffman would retreat to his study. Since he'd lost his father last year, Kevin was sure they were still grieving for their only son, Billy, who'd died from a football injury. But it didn't help matters for Bridget, who was homesick for Ireland.

"I really do like to cook," Bridget told Mrs. Lambart, "and Mrs. Hoffman doesn't seem to mind my bringing dishes over."

"If you'll tell me what ingredients you need, I can buy them," she answered, "and you can come over here to do the cooking."

Bridget glanced at Kevin tentatively. "Well, I wouldn't want to be a nuisance."

"Nonsense, my dear. Who's going to complain about excellent cooking? Besides, it will give the two of you a chance to talk about your homeland." Mrs. Lambart turned to Kevin. "Wouldn't that be nice?"

Kevin struggled to keep his face impassive. After his father's accident last year, his mother and sister had kept themselves busy by cooking frantically. He didn't understand why, but the activity seemed to help them. Bridget had told him cooking Irish food made her feel connected to home, so how could he say anything?

He forced another smile and nodded, for once grateful he didn't have to speak right now. If Wendy found out Bridget would be coming over to cook—even just once in a while—would she get the wrong impression? He wasn't dating Bridget and she had no expectations that he would. But would Wendy understand?

Worse, would Wendy even care? She'd been invited to stay for lunch and she declined. If she liked him—the way he wanted her to—wouldn't she have stayed?

The thoughts swirled around in his mind until his head felt like he'd mixed too much whiskey into an Irish coffee.

He wished James were here to talk to because he didn't think he'd ever understand girls.

****

"Where are we going?" Wendy asked as Jo drove past their yard road. "I don't feel like visiting anyone."

"No worries," Jo said as she turned down a field road and parked the car. "I thought we might walk to the old cabin."

"The cabin? I haven't been there in probably a year."

"Me either," Jo said, "but if your mom sees you with those red eyes, she'll want to know why you've been crying…and you know she won't stop until she gets an answer."

"That's true." Wendy got out of the car and led the way through the grassy ditch and into the woods behind their farmhouse.

Jo caught up with her. "It's a safe place to get your head together."

They walked in silence as they followed a narrow deer trail through the underbrush. They rounded a stand of evergreens and stopped when the small stone hut with a lean-to came into view. "Remember the first time you came to visit us and saw the cabin?"

"I remember nearly jumping out of my skin when you went to get firewood and I heard the wolf howl." Jo shook her head. "I was really mad when I found out it was you trying to scare me."

Wendy grimaced. "Yeah, well. We were only thirteen."

Jo opened the door and they stepped inside. "I hope no furry creatures are calling this home now."

Wendy smiled in spite of her bad mood. "If there are, I won't leave you with them this time."

The place looked much as it had the last time she'd been here. A large hearth took up most of one wall. Oil lamps hung on either side of it. A small cupboard over a counter that held a washbasin stood against one wall, while an Army-style cot lined another. The wooden table and two chairs were still there, too. In spite of not having been used, it looked relatively clean—and furry-creature free.

Jo pulled out one of the chairs. "I remember you said you and Luke would come here. I thought maybe you two were a thing."

Wendy took the other chair. "I was just trying to make you jealous. You'd just gotten here and Luke was already paying attention to you."

"I felt awful, thinking you had a crush on him too."

"We were pretty silly, weren't we?"

"As you said, we were only thirteen." Jo frowned. "It was different when I came back two years later and Luke was dating Amy Patterson."

"I'd almost forgotten about that."

"It's history now," Jo agreed, "but at the time, I was devastated. The worst thing about it was that Amy was so *nice*."

Wendy looked at her. "Kind of like Bridget?"

"Yeah, kind of." Jo hesitated. "You don't know for sure that Kevin wants to date Bridget."

"She sure is over at his place a lot if he doesn't," Wendy said. "And she cooks. Really *cooks*. I'm lucky if I don't start a fire frying a hamburger. I can't compete with that."

"Don't put yourself down. Not every girl *likes* to cook."

"Yeah, but every guy likes to eat," Wendy answered. "Just look at my mom and Luke's dad. He comes over with Luke for Thanksgiving dinner and *voilà*! He's following my mom around like a puppy."

"That's different. Your mom's a widow, he's a widower. They probably are both lonely and like the companionship."

"Maybe. But I'll bet Bridget wants more than that."

"I'm not so sure. She mentions Ireland a lot. Kevin can relate."

Wendy frowned. "You don't need to remind me of that."

"Sorry. I didn't mean it that way. I meant *friends* share things in common."

"I don't think you're helping here." Wendy shrugged. "But I probably should've stayed for lunch and held my ground."

"I know it's hard, but try not to think of it as a battle," Jo said. "I was so wrong about Amy."

"That's because Luke realized he liked you best."

"But that didn't happen right away."

"Yes, but he *told* you he was breaking off with Amy. Kevin hasn't said anything like that."

"Do you know how un-sensible that sounds? I'm sorry," she added, stifling a laugh when Wendy glared at her. "He can't say he's *breaking off* with Bridget when he's not even dating her."

Wendy stuck her chin out mulishly. "Still."

"Okay." Jo got up and shoved the chair back in. "When we start riding again, why don't you bring Kevin to the cabin? He's not seen it."

Wendy rose too. "He'll think I'm coming on to him."

Jo rolled her eyes. "Isn't that kind of the point?"

"But what if he says no? Or tells me he just wants to be friends?"

Jo studied her for a moment. "Then you won't have to cry anymore. You'll know where you stand."

"But…" Wendy snapped her mouth shut. Her cousin was right. She couldn't keep on crying and getting upset all the time.

But…the truth was, did she really want to know where she stood with Kevin?

Chapter Eleven

Kevin returned to school the following Monday. Regardless of what Jo had said, Wendy was still not sure how to go about finding out where things stood. But by the time she saw him in Government class, two news items had taken priority.

The first was a mass killing at a small village in Vietnam called My Lai.

The second was that Robert Kennedy, favoring peace talks over continued war, had decided to run in the Democratic primary.

"I think Robert Kennedy is right," Mark said. "We need to stop fighting their war for them."

"He didn't say that," Mr. Kyle replied. "He wants to negotiate an agreement to cease fire, period."

"If they don't end up killing each other first," another student said. "The north Vietnamese just killed hundreds of south Vietnamese at that My Lai place, including women and kids."

"Um, the news reports didn't say it was Viet Cong that did it." Mr. Kyle looked around the room, letting that information sink in.

"Well, who else would do it?" a girl asked.

"No one is sure. There's rumor it was friendly fire," Mr. Kyle replied.

"Like they turned on their own?" Dwayne asked.

"Not the Vietnamese."

Cynthia Breeding

Wendy's eyes widened. "You mean *our* Army might have had something to do with it?"

Mr. Kyle hesitated. "It's only speculation, but that has been floated."

"That's impossible!" Wendy sputtered. "How could our soldiers do something like that?"

"They've been taught to kill," Mark said. "That's what happens in the Army."

"Like you would know," Tommy said. "You're going to run off to Canada."

"And be a draft dodger!" Tim added.

"That's enough," Mr. Kyle said. "We don't need to be accusing each other of things."

"Right," Lionel muttered. "Like there's already enough killing on the streets."

Wendy gave him a startled look. "Not *here*."

"I meant Detroit."

"All big cities have crime," Dwayne said, "but it usually happens in the poor neighborhoods."

Lionel shot him a belligerent look. "Are you saying I'm poor?"

"Enough," Mr. Kyle said again. "Crime can happen anywhere, in any neighborhood. Any country, even. Kevin can probably attest to the unease in Ireland right now."

Kevin made an attempt to speak, but he sounded more like he was barking. Bridget gave him a quick look and spoke up.

"Aye, there's been problems," she said, "but 'tis mainly with Ireland wanting the north to break away from the U.K."

"I thought it was about religion," Mark said. "Irish Catholics don't like Protestants."

Kevin coughed and tried to speak. "'Tis more that there's discrimination…" His voice went raspy. "…with the Catholics not getting hired or finding housing in the north—" He succumbed to another fit of coughing.

"Go get some water," Mr. Kyle said.

Wendy watched as Kevin nearly ran from the room. Any questions she had for him or talking to him would have to wait. Which might be a good idea, considering the longer she postponed confronting her dilemma, it *might* work itself out.

She could almost hear Jo laughing at such a flimsy excuse, but she really didn't want to face rejection, either. She forced herself to pay attention to the class discussion, which by now had taken a turn to unrest in Germany and France and clashes between Israel and Jordan as well as hints of revolution in the Middle East.

Wendy shut her eyes, as if closing them would keep her from hearing about all the trouble that seemed to be happening everywhere. They might be safe in Middletown, Minnesota, but would it last or would dissent rear its ugly head here too?

From the way the class was arguing, she felt it was already starting to happen.

****

After a week of thawing temperatures that melted most of the snow and turned everything to slushy mud, Saturday at the beginning of Spring Break dawned clear and sunny with an almost warm breeze. Wendy was more than ready to get the horses out, even if they had to stay on the graveled roads. Even better, Kevin had recovered and ridden over to join them. She was hoping they'd have time to spend together over the break.

Unfortunately, the twins arrived a few minutes later,

which meant her chances for any kind of private conversation with Kevin had just disappeared like the snowbanks.

Tommy watched her coil her rope and attach it to a leather strap. "Planning to lasso someone?"

Wendy's face heated. What would Kevin think about that kind of remark? Blast her cousin. "Maybe I'll practice on you."

He grinned wickedly. "You know I'm not the one you want—"

"Never mind!" Wendy sprang into the saddle, hurriedly changing the subject. "I think I smell spring."

Tim laughed. "You can't *smell* spring."

"Sure you can," Wendy answered. "It smells...*fresh*."

"You can't smell fresh, either," Tommy chortled.

"I ken what Wendy means, though." Kevin brought his horse alongside hers. "In Ireland in the spring, the grass is greener, the sun brighter, the sky bluer."

Wendy threw her cousins a triumphant look. "There. You see?"

"Doesn't it rain nearly every day?" Jo asked.

"Aye," Kevin answered, "but that also gives us rainbows. Ireland has some of the grandest rainbows ye've ever seen."

Tommy snickered again. "Along with pots of gold?"

"And don't tell us there are leprechauns, too," Tim added.

Kevin cast him a sideways look. "'Tis a sayin' in Ireland that if ye don't believe in the little people, they'll prove ye wrong."

"Superstition," Tommy said.

Kevin shrugged. "Perhaps."

"Like what are they going to do?" Tim asked. "Knock us off our horses?"

"Or maybe make us trip and fall?" Tommy joined in the teasing.

Kevin shook his head. "Ye would be wise nae to tempt the Fae."

Tim lifted an eyebrow. "Are you really that superstitious?"

Tommy smirked. "Yeah, it's not like leprechauns or little people or faeries are real."

"Enough bickering," Jo said. "Let's enjoy the day."

"Yes, let's," Wendy agreed.

The twins rolled their eyes, then urged their horses forward and they all rode in companionable silence for a while before Wendy realized they were headed toward the old bridge where she and Jo had ridden with Kevin before.

"Are we headed toward the cave?"

"It'll be too slippery to climb up there," Jo said quickly.

"You don't have to go," Tommy said. "You can wait on this side of the river."

"But why do you want to go over there at all?" Wendy asked.

The twins grinned at each other. "We want to check it out. See what it needs."

"What it needs?" Wendy drew her brows together. "It's just a place with a bunch of bad memories."

"Not for us," Tim said. "We're thinking, with maybe a little furnishing, it'll be a good place for some privacy with our girlfriends."

"You're crazy."

"Crazy-smart," Tommy said. "We almost got caught

at the drive-in movie steaming up the windows last fall."

Tim nodded. "Dad would ground us for sure if the local cop followed us home."

"You'll be in even bigger trouble with Susan and Carla's dads if they find out," Wendy warned.

"That's just it," Tim replied. "They *won't* find out, as far away from town as the cave is. We know how to plan."

"They're both stupid," Wendy muttered several minutes later when everyone had tethered their horses and the twins had walked across the rickety bridge to the other side.

Jo looked away as they started crawling over the boulders toward the cave near the top. "I think I'm going for a walk." She gave the twins a quick glance and then turned around. "In the other direction."

Wendy wasn't sure if Jo was really all that upset being so near the cave or if she was using it as an excuse to give her some time alone with Kevin. Either way, she wasn't going to argue.

Kevin pointed. "That rock over there has had the sun shinin' on it for a while. It should be dry. You want to try that?"

"Sure," Wendy said, making her way over. The rock was big enough for both of them to sit on, although it didn't leave much room for separation. Not that she minded as Kevin sat down beside her, his thigh brushing hers. She resisted the urge to lean on him.

Kevin looked around the rocky outcrops that lined either side of the narrow banks along the river and then to the trees beyond. "You're probably goin' to laugh at me, but this place feels creepy, almost looks like it could be haunted."

"I won't laugh." Wendy smiled. "Actually, you might be right. There's kind of a legend about this place."

"A legend?"

"Kind of. About twenty-five years ago, a couple of teenagers ran off together. They were going to elope, but their car veered off the bridge and crashed into the river. The girl drowned. The boy survived."

"How sad. What happened to him?"

"He moved away." Wendy looked toward the rushing river. "But the legend goes that on the anniversary of that crash, you can hear the girl crying from the water."

"Do ye believe in ghosts, then?"

Wendy shrugged. "I don't know that I *don't* believe. There were times after my father died that I thought he was talking to me in my dreams."

"Maybe he was."

"Maybe." Wendy smiled. "He seemed to be lecturing me a lot in those dreams."

"Lecturin'?"

"Yeah, like telling me not to get into trouble, not to make my mother worry and…" Wendy hesitated.

"And?"

"…it sounds stupid, but he'd call me princess and say one day I'd…" She paused again and took a deep breath. "…that I'd find my Prince Charming."

Kevin studied her. "Ye are lookin' for Prince Charmin'?"

"No, of course not. That's just a fairy tale." Wendy tried not to squirm under Kevin's direct look. "I mean, when I saw *Camelot,* I thought a knight in shining armor would be cool, but that's just wishful thinking."

He was quiet for a moment. "Did ye think James was your knight in shinin' armor?"

Wendy blinked, suddenly remembering the letter that Kevin had written when he'd gone back to Ireland last year. "You just can't let that rest, can you?"

Kevin blinked too. "Let what rest?"

Wendy frowned. "You know. You basically told me I was making a fool of myself."

"I did nae say that."

"You implied it." Wendy started to feel the embarrassment all over again and, with it, a bit of temper as well. "You said I should realize when someone is in love with someone else. And that it was a waste of time to try and force someone to like someone. Like you were the big expert. Well, I figured out that James was crazy about Mary Anne. Maybe it took me a little longer than it should have—"

"I didn't mean..." Kevin stopped talking as Jo returned from her walk. "I'll explain later."

Wendy shook her head. "You don't have to explain anything. I got the message. Let's just forget it."

"Forget what?" Jo asked as she joined them.

"Nothing," Wendy answered and then pointed across the river. "The twins are coming back down."

"I hope they cross over one at a time." Jo looked worried. "What's left of that bridge is pretty rickety."

"It should hold if they're careful." Wendy looked up at the sky as the wind suddenly started to gust, causing the leafless branches to stir. "It's not supposed to storm today, is it?"

"No." Jo looked up at the sky too. "Besides, there aren't any clouds."

Wendy tilted her head at the sudden creaking sound

114

from the old bridge. Tim was halfway across and Tommy was right behind him. "They're making the bridge sway!"

"'Tis nae them, I think. 'Tis an unnatural wind." Kevin jumped up as one of the boards cracked.

"What do you mean?" Jo asked.

"The bridge really isn't haunted," Wendy added, "in spite of the stories."

"No ghosties. 'Tis the Fae, I suspect," Kevin answered. "They don't like being made fun of."

"But that's…" Jo stopped as another board cracked and all three of them watched in horror as Tim and Tommy both teetered on the splintered wood for a long moment.

They grabbed each other for balance and then they toppled over together.

Kevin ran toward the river as the twins landed with a loud splash in the rushing water.

Chapter Twelve

Although he was used to swimming in the cold Atlantic off Ireland's west coast, Kevin still felt the momentary shock of the frigid river as he plunged in. Immediately he forced all of his limbs into action because he knew they would grow numb in seconds if he didn't. The twins were being swept completely under the water time after time, proof that their arms were already incapable of movement. Their faces emerged briefly and they managed to spit out water before sinking below the surface again.

Kevin sighted a bend in the river where it narrowed to circumvent several boulders. Using powerful strokes to stay out of the main current and closer to the shore, he swam toward it. Trying to catch the twins in the fast-flowing water would be easier to do if he could get ahead of them and create a human barrier.

Above the roar of the river, he could hear Wendy and Jo shouting from the bank. "We've got the rope!" one of them yelled.

He didn't have the energy to spare in response, but in his peripheral vision he glimpsed them running alongside, Wendy coiling the rope she'd taken from her saddle. He remembered how the twins had teased her about playing cowgirl by having it attached, but he had no time to dwell on the irony of it. The twins were almost abreast of him, floating face down now, and he hadn't reached the bend. If they got past that, he didn't know if he'd be able to catch them. With an effort, he kicked harder even though he was losing feeling in his legs as well.

When his foot contacted something hard, it took a moment to realize he'd hit the bottom of one of the boulders below the surface. Pushing off from that gave him the momentum he needed to reach the bend just before the twins' bodies did. Bracing his back against the rock that jutted out, he managed to throw out an arm to halt them. He breathed a sigh of relief when they both caught his arm and sputtered.

"I've got you." Quickly Kevin pulled his belt from his jeans with his other arm and lashed their wrists, binding them together. "Don't fight me." He didn't think they had the strength, but drowning victims often acted out of sheer survival instinct and his own stamina was rapidly fading. "Don't fight me."

"I'm going to throw my rope," Wendy yelled from the bank. "Are you ready?"

"Tie the other end to a bush first," he managed to shout back and was thankful when Jo nodded and ran to do what he asked. The last thing he needed was for one or both girls to fall into the water trying to pull the three of them out. "We're steady here." While that was true, the boulder keeping them from being swept downstream, the inactivity was also paralyzing his own arms. He lifted one out of the water while hanging on to his makeshift leather tether with the other. At least, he hoped he was still hanging on to it. There was no feeling in that hand.

"Here it comes!" Wendy threw the line. It snaked over the water and then fell, inches short of where he could reach it.

"Try again!" By the saints, the water was freezing…

Wendy muttered something that sounded a lot like a curse as she pulled the rope back in, quickly recoiling it for a second throw.

"Hang on!" Jo shouted.

"Here it comes!" Wendy tossed the rope again, half-spinning as she used her weight behind the throw.

This time the rope sailed over his head, part of it whipping against his face as he managed to catch it. He ignored the pain. That it stung at all was a good sign.

"Got it!" Thankfully, she'd made a wide loop at the end that he managed to pull over one shoulder and arm. He adjusted his hold on the leather wrist tether, bringing the twins in closer. He placed their free hands on the rope and hoped they had the strength to hold on. "Okay! Pull!"

Jo stood behind Wendy and they synchronized their moves much as rowers would, and slowly Kevin could feel the three of them being floated toward the shore. "Hang on," he said to Tim and Tommy. "We're almost there."

Then his heart nearly stopped as Wendy slipped and fell on her bottom. For one horrified moment, he watched as she began to slide down toward the water.

"Hang on to the rope!" he yelled to her. "Don't let go!"

Whether she heard him or not, he didn't know, but she started to scramble for purchase and managed to crawl back up to where she could use the bush to regain her standing. The rope grew taut again and he felt them moving forward once more.

In what felt like an eternity, but was probably less than a minute or two later, his feet hit the rocky shallows near the banks. Somehow—perhaps the Fae were feeling merciful—the twins managed to find their footing and all three of them staggered out of the water to collapse on solid ground.

"Oh, my God!" Wendy sank down beside him and tugged him onto her lap, wrapping her arms around him. "I thought you'd drown!" She hugged him tighter. "I don't know what I would have done if something had happened to you!"

A part of him knew she was reacting to the danger of the situation, that it was just fear talking, but she felt so good and so *warm*.

"Hold me, please."

"I am." She stroked his wet hair, then held him close again. "I am."

He closed his eyes to bask in that, at least for a minute.

****

"Can you hear me?" Wendy touched Kevin's shoulder gently. "Can you wake up? Please?"

Slowly, his eyelids fluttered open, his gaze unfocused at first and then sharpening as he looked around. "Where am I?"

"You're in a guest room at Tim and Tommy's," Wendy replied. "Their dad brought all three of you here."

"They're all right? They made it?"

"They made it," Wendy replied. "The doctor put both of them to bed."

"Doctor? How long have I been out?"

"Only about an hour. The doctor said you were exhausted and to let you sleep."

Kevin started to get up, but Mrs. Lambart bustled

over. "Just lie still, dear. You nearly killed yourself. I came over as soon as I heard."

He managed to prop himself against the headboard. "I remember collapsin' on the river bank. What happened after that?"

Wendy bit her lip. He didn't remember her holding him? Or his *asking* her to? Even though she'd never been so scared in her life, that moment had felt so good. Cold and shaking as he was, she'd felt a bond when she'd wrapped her arms around him and he'd dropped his head on her lap. But he didn't seem to recall it. She would do well not to bring it up, then.

"Jo rode Silver home to get help. I used the saddle blankets to try and keep you guys warm," she said. "It seemed like forever before I heard the truck coming, but it was probably only fifteen minutes or so."

"Were all three of us out?"

Wendy nodded. "The twins collapsed right after you did."

Kevin's eyes studied her. "So ye were all alone, hopin' we weren't all dead? It must have been a long fifteen minutes."

"You were all breathing, but you were so *cold*. And the twins' lips were blue." Wendy gave him a shaky smile. "It was pretty scary."

"I'm sorry."

She felt her eyes widen. "Why are you apologizing? You saved Tim and Tommy's lives. You're a hero."

"I just did what anyone who's a strong swimmer would do. I'm sorry for scarin' ye though." Kevin hesitated. "And thanks for stayin' with us."

Did he think she wouldn't stay with him? Wendy frowned. He'd said "stayin' with us." *Us*. Since he'd passed out, he probably thought she'd just watched all of them instead of trying to keep him extra warm. Well, he might not remember, but she always would. That would suffice for now.

"Silver is the fastest horse," she said, "and he only lets Jo ride him, so I stayed with you guys."

"I'm glad you…" Kevin stopped to sneeze. "…did." He sneezed again.

Mrs. Lambart came to the side of the bed and put her hand on his forehead. "I hope you aren't going to get sick again."

"Me too."

"The doctor left antibiotics for all three of you," Wendy said. "Just in case."

"And he ordered all three of you to stay in bed for several days and then not to go outside for a week," Mrs. Lambart said. "It's a good thing it's Spring Break so you won't miss school."

Wendy felt a hysterical bubble rise in her throat. She was pretty sure the twins wouldn't see that as a good thing. She didn't like the idea either, since she'd hoped they'd get to do a lot of horseback riding and maybe go to the cabin.

"But I'll have to go outside just to get back home."

Mrs. Lambart patted his hand. "I'm glad you think of our place as your home, but the twins' parents insist you stay right here until you're well."

"But I'm imposin'."

"I doubt they would think that, since you just saved their sons from drowning," she said. "In fact, they are waiting to come up and talk to you."

"Jo and my mom are waiting too." Wendy paused. "So is Bridget."

"Bridget? How did she find out?"

Was that a spark of interest in his eyes? Wendy forced her facial expression to remain neutral. "She was over at the Lambarts' when my mom called."

"Oh." He smiled at Mrs. Lambart. "Another Irish cookin' lesson?"

She smiled back. "Scones, this time. She said they go best with strawberry jam and clotted cream."

"They do."

"Well, I'll bring you some when I come back, then. Right now, I'd better let everyone know you're awake." She turned to Wendy. "Want to walk down with me?"

She didn't, but she reluctantly nodded. She wanted to stay, but it would sound really weird if she said that. And the room would be crowded with five people.

"I'll come back tomorrow, okay?"

"That will be good."

"Well, okay, then. Until tomorrow." She felt like she was prattling as she followed Mrs. Lambart out the door. At least, coming to her cousins' house was a natural thing to do, so it wouldn't seem like she was *just* visiting Kevin. And then another thought almost made her smile.

If Kevin were staying here, Bridget wouldn't be bringing over casseroles.

She hoped.

****

By the time school resumed the Monday after Spring Break, the twins and Kevin had fully recovered. He didn't think he'd ever been so glad to get back to the routine of school in his life. Staying in bed the first couple of days hadn't been a problem since he'd been totally exhausted after the ordeal, but the remaining part of the week made him feel like a caged lion who wanted to roar.

Not that everyone hadn't been kind and helpful. They were. He'd even made headlines in the weekly newspaper. Everyone from the local police chief to the parson had called him a hero, which embarrassed him to no end. The twins' mother had barely allowed him to lift a finger to do anything, even to buttering his morning toast and making sure his eggs were cooked just like he wanted them. Thank the saints, the Wades didn't employ servants or someone probably would have helped dress him, too.

At least half the students—mostly girls—had also found their way to the farm. Mrs. Wade had turned most of them away, saying everyone needed their rest. It was probably as much to give Tim and Tommy time to recover from their battered egos as well as their physical bruises. Colonel Wade had given them a long, stern lecture on being foolish enough to get on the old bridge and had grounded them for a month. At least, their father didn't know the real reason why the twins had done it. They might have been grounded until graduation.

Bridget and Wendy had come over several times— Bridget usually bringing scones, since Mrs. Wade had developed a liking for them—and Wendy just bringing herself. Their conversations focused on what the other kids were doing over Spring Break and, unlike everyone else, she didn't talk about what had happened. He was grateful for that until he realized she hadn't mentioned holding him, either.

Could she have forgotten? He didn't see how, since *he* remembered every instant—at least until he passed out—vividly. How she had wrapped her arms around him, pulled him closer, brushed his wet hair back… Even now he could feel the warmth of her body as he lay in her lap, and the light scent of the skin lotion she used. And she had *said*—he was almost a hundred percent sure—that she wouldn't know what she would do if something happened to him. She had said it, hadn't she? He hoped he hadn't been delirious. But…she hadn't mentioned it since then.

Uncertainty was driving him crazy.

He didn't much like the fact, either, that Wendy was already engrossed in conversation with Dwayne as they gathered at their project table in Government. He was telling her about going to Palm Beach for Spring Break and she was complimenting him on the tan he'd acquired.

Kevin wondered if Wendy was ignoring him or if she was still upset. Although the subject hadn't come up while he was recuperating, they'd been on the brink of an argument about that stupid letter he'd written her when Jo returned from her walk that Saturday. In retrospect, he probably shouldn't have written it, considering he was guilty of the very same thing—being besotted with someone…*her*—that he was accusing her of.

"So the hero returns triumphant," Dwayne said as Kevin sat down. "I half-expected to see you wearing a bunch of medals."

Kevin thought he detected a note of sarcasm, but before he could answer, Bridget spoke up.

"He is a hero, just like one of King Arthur's knights!"

Wendy gave her a sharp look. "You like the King Arthur legends?"

"Of course. We Irish claim Tristan, ye know."

Bridget gave Kevin a big smile. "And ye were every inch as brave."

Kevin tried not to squirm. "I'm no knight."

"You could have fooled me," Dwayne said.

"It really doesn't matter what you think," Tommy cut in as he walked toward their table. "Kevin saved our lives."

Tim came to stand beside his twin. "And nobody better insult him."

As if sensing a fight about to break out, Wendy quickly changed the subject. "I guess you guys won't be going up to the cave anymore."

Tommy shrugged. "Well, we can always get there by using the new bridge."

"It's only half a mile down the road from the old one," Tim added. "Susan and Carla still want to see the cave."

Wendy shook her head. "Do the two of you only share one brain cell?"

"Hey." Tommy looked affronted. "It's not like we're going to take any more risks."

"Yeah, we learned *that* lesson," Tim said.

"That cave is bad luck," Wendy said. "Just stay away from it."

Dwayne gave her a speculative look, his interest in goading Kevin apparently forgotten. He would need to thank her later for diverting attention away from him. The last thing he needed was a stupid fight.

"Where is this cave?" Dwayne asked.

"It's down by the river, hidden amongst some boulders," Wendy answered.

"Why is it bad luck to go there?"

"It's a long story," Wendy said, "but my sister got

abducted three years ago and when my cousin Jo tried to follow her, she got caught too. They were both taken to that cave."

"But everything turned out okay," Tommy said, "so it's not really unlucky after all."

Tim nodded. "Yeah, our girlfriends thought it might even be romantic."

Wendy rolled her eyes. "I'm not sure you two even have a single brain cell."

Kevin tended to agree with her. The twins were still the twins.

****

The next afternoon, Dwayne drove one of his father's rental cars over the new bridge and turned onto the rutted lane that led to an outcropping of rocks close to the river. Seeing the conditions of the so-called road, he'd been smart not to drive his Camaro. But then, he knew he was smart.

He parked the car and got out, looking over the rocky outcrop bordering the river, searching for the entrance to the cave. He'd casually asked around about the old bridge—everyone was eager to talk about what had happened—so he had a pretty good idea of the location.

He'd also learned of the legend of the lovers who'd met their fate. He'd almost laughed out loud at how seriously these idiots took the story, but then, what else did they do for excitement in these hick towns? A couple of the girls had even gotten all sappy and romantic about it, quoting lines from the song "Teen Angel."

How stupid.

He spotted what looked like a dark hole in the boulders and started to climb. The only girl—person—

who wasn't totally stupid in this town was Wendy Wade. *She*, at least, appreciated his intelligence.

And, he was pretty sure, she was interested in him. Why else was she always smiling at him and giving him compliments? And she asked him lots of questions, too, which just proved she knew he was smarter than the rest of those bozos, including the dorky twins and that Irish sod who ran around playing hero.

He reached the flat top of the rock where the cave entrance was. Stepping inside, he peered around. It was roomier than he expected. It certainly would accommodate two.

Stepping back into the sunlight, he smiled. Wendy had chosen well when she'd chosen him. She might be somewhat naïve and most likely a virgin, but he could be accommodating. When he'd met with a drug dealer in Miami, he'd gotten both 'ludes and Ecstasy. And he had a couple of acid-laced postage stamps, as well.

He'd finally found someone who liked him and shared his interests. He would take her on the trip of her life.

And this cave would be the perfect place to do it.

Chapter Thirteen

"Spring is definitely in the air!" Wendy looked at the tiny bits of green budding from the trees as she and Jo cantered down the road to meet up with the rest of the Hill Riders for their first official Saturday outing.

"Well, Monday is the first of April," Jo answered. "I just hope we don't get a late winter snowstorm like a couple of years ago."

"We won't." Wendy patted Jupiter's neck. "I have a feeling we're going to have a wonderful spring this year!"

Jo grinned. "That's because you're smitten with Kevin."

"I am not!" Wendy felt herself blush.

"Oh, come on. You've got to admit he really played the knight, although it was good he wasn't wearing armor—he would have sunk."

Wendy smiled at her joke. "Yeah, and now every girl at school thinks he's really cool. It's not just Bridget I have to worry about."

Jo gave her a quick glance. "I don't think you've ever had to really worry about Bridget."

Wendy made a face at her cousin. "Says you. She cooks and bakes and has both Mrs. Lambart and my aunt wrapped around her little finger."

"That doesn't mean Kevin is."

"Didn't you hear me? Bridget *cooks* and *bakes*

everything that Kevin likes. Remember what our Home Ec teachers said? The way to a man's heart is through his stomach."

Jo shook her head. "I don't cook for Luke and he doesn't care."

"He's in college, silly. How could you cook for him?"

"You know what I mean."

Wendy relented. "Yeah, I guess I do. It's just that…Bridget is from Ireland too—"

"And homesick," Jo said. "She's admitted that. Kevin is just being a friend."

Wendy hoped her cousin was right. Kevin didn't act like he was smitten with Bridget, but then he didn't act like he was smitten with *her* either. And since the accident, there were always other girls hanging around too. She sighed.

"Stop being so moody," Jo said. "It's spring, remember? The time to look forward to everything coming to life again."

"That's true." Wendy shook off her dismal feelings. "I saw a robin the other day. That's always a sign of good things to come."

"Exactly," Jo replied. "Spring is the time for good things to happen."

****

The pleasant weekend weather carried over, and by Thursday, students were restless for having to stay indoors.

"Easter is just around the corner." Tommy slid into his seat beside Wendy in Government class. "Why don't you take Kevin on an Easter egg hunt?"

Thankfully, Kevin hadn't come into the room yet.

Wendy rolled her eyes. "Isn't that a little childish?"

Tim grinned as he sat down behind her. "Not if you put on bunny ears and pretend to be—"

"*Hush!*" Hopefully, the other students coming in were making too much noise for him to be heard. She was pretty sure her face was as bright a pink as any Easter egg.

"You could make a trail that leads to the cabin," Tim continued as though she hadn't spoken, "and then you could be alone with him."

"*HUSH!*"

Everyone stilled as students turned to look at her. Wendy closed her eyes as though that would make everyone go away. She hadn't intended to shout. Her cousins really did deserve to be dunked in the cold river again.

"I am assuming Miss Wade was directing her remark toward Tim," Mr. Kyle said, "but it is an excellent suggestion. Everyone, please be seated."

Bless her teacher. She heard rustling as students began to move again and slowly opened her eyes. Kevin was giving her a curious look. He must have come in while she was trying to disappear. She only hoped he hadn't heard anything besides her hushing Tim. Her face warmed at the mortification and then heated further as she thought about being alone with Kevin at the cabin.

It was a cozy place. There would be dry firewood in the bin next to the hearth and a supply of candles along with the oil lamps. She could take a blanket to spread in front of the fireplace and, since it was Easter, maybe take some egg salad sandwiches…

Stop it. Wendy gave herself an inner shake. What was she thinking? What would *Kevin* think if she lured him to such an isolated spot? Strangely, instead of feeling even more mortified at such a thing, the thought made her suddenly feel overly warm. And she had the strangest tingling sensation running down her spine.

Tim gave her a poke. "Daydreaming?"

She turned around to glare at him. "I am *not*. Stop bugging me—"

"I just wanted you to pass the worksheets back."

"Worksheets? Oh." Wendy frowned as she saw the student ahead of her patiently holding them out. She took the stack. "Sorry."

"All right, class," Mr. Kyle said. "Since President Johnson announced he won't be seeking re-election and Robert Kennedy has declared he will run for the office, I want each of you to rank in order what qualities you think most important that the new president should have. We'll discuss your opinions tomorrow."

Wendy found herself doodling, drawing Easter eggs and baskets and bunnies and thinking of the most important attributes in a relationship instead of the presidency. When she realized she was sketching the cabin, she sighed and put her pencil down.

She would have to concentrate on coming up with some good answers later since she didn't think Mr. Kyle would appreciate her artwork when she turned in the assignment tomorrow.

But then, by tomorrow, they would be focusing on something much more important.

****

Wendy felt horrible Friday morning. She had spoken too soon about a great spring. An eerie, stunned silence had filled most of the classrooms and only footsteps were heard in the halls.

Cynthia Breeding

Dr. Martin Luther King had been murdered the night before.

Still shell-shocked, students filed quietly into Government class. Just one more period to go before the weekend arrived and she could go home to try and make sense of it all.

And how ironic that this would be Palm Sunday. Dr King had just made a speech about being to the mountaintop and having seen the victory. It reminded Wendy of the triumphant march Jesus had made into Jerusalem prior to his own betrayal.

How could Dr. King have been so close to success, only to have his life snuffed out by an assassin's bullet?

Mr. Kyle looked around the room of somber faces. "For what it's worth, every one of you is seeing—feeling—history being made."

"It doesn't make sense," Tommy said, his countenance, for once, serious.

"Yeah, why would someone shoot Dr. King?" Tim asked, his voice equally serious.

"'Cuz white folks don't like blacks," Lionel said.

"That's not true!" Wendy wiped at tears. "What difference does it make what color you are?"

"You are both right," Mr. Kyle said. "It shouldn't make any difference. All humans should have equal rights." He sighed heavily. "Unfortunately, there are those who can't accept that idea."

Lionel thrust out his chin. "That still don't make it right."

"I didn't say it did," their teacher answered, "but hate is not logical."

Dwayne narrowed his gaze at Lionel. "Your people hate too. Riots broke out all over the country last night."

Lionel glared back. "What do you expect us to do? Lie down like dogs and take it? We aren't slaves anymore."

"So you set fires, broke into buildings, and looted?"

Lionel shrugged. "Maybe the Black Panthers are right. We need to be more aggressive."

"Let's direct this discussion to the current situation," Mr. Kyle said. "Dr. King advocated non-violence. He wouldn't have approved of all the carnage."

"Senator Kennedy managed to keep Indianapolis from rioting last night," Mark said. "At least that's something."

"It's just so sad," Wendy said. "I loved Dr. King's *I have a dream* speech."

"Yes, that was five years ago," Mr. Kyle said, "and the Civil Rights movement has come a long way since then. Maybe not at the speed we'd hoped for, but strides have been made, in spite of what just happened."

"We just need to remember that dream," Mark said. "If Robert Kennedy is elected, he'll make it happen."

"Maybe." Lionel shook his head. "But you're the one who's dreamin' if you think this will blow over. The trouble's just begun."

****

Lionel's dire prediction turned out to be more than true. Wendy felt depressed by the time she took her seat in Government the following Thursday. A whole week had passed. Even though President Johnson was supposed to sign a second Civil Rights Bill today, riots had broken out in more than a hundred cities since the assassination and, along with numerous arrests and injuries, a shootout between Black Panthers and police had gotten a seventeen-year-old killed and just upped the ante for more violence.

It hardly seemed like this was going to be Easter weekend, which was supposed to be about redemption and salvation. From the horrible nightly news, America seemed a far cry from achieving anything close to that.

If there was any kind of redeeming quality to the current situation, it was that the problems in Vietnam had taken a back seat. At least, temporarily.

"Man," Mark said as he came in holding a copy of the *Atlanta Journal-Constitution.* "It says here that Dr. King's funeral procession was three and a half miles long, with over one hundred thousand people along the way and no fights." He looked at Mr. Kyle. "Do you think there's hope for us?"

The teacher gave him a brief smile. "There's always hope."

"Something good has to come out of this," Wendy said. "It just has to. I don't want bad things to keep happening."

As the class started discussing Mark's article, Dwayne leaned toward her to whisper. "There are ways to make you forget about all this and feel good."

Wendy frowned. "Like what?"

He smiled. "Can't tell you here. Maybe we can meet over the weekend?"

"I…" Wendy hesitated. She didn't want to discourage Dwayne from being a friend, since he was finally starting to open up a little, but she didn't want him to think she was interested in going on a date. "I…I'll have to check with my mother. We usually put Easter baskets together for the church to give out."

Dwayne gave her a thoughtful look. "You really are one of a kind, aren't you?"

She wasn't sure how to take that, so she shrugged. "I guess."

"Well, I *know* you are."

Mr. Kyle cleared his throat, a clear signal the whispering should stop. Wendy gave him her full attention. The last thing she needed was for Kevin to think she was sharing secrets with Dwayne.

"I found something this week that I thought some of you might be interested in." Mr. Kyle held up a pamphlet. "Everyone's heard of the Peace Corps, right? Well, you have to be an adult, preferably with a degree, to get into that, but there's a program for teens that's associated with it. It's called Global Leadership Adventures and lets you volunteer to go to developing countries for several weeks in the summer."

"Like where?" Tommy asked.

He looked at the pamphlet. "It says here sixteen countries throughout Asia, Africa, Europe and Latin America."

Tim tilted his head. "What would we do?"

"Things like learning a different culture, getting to know locals, even meet with leaders in communities and helping out." Mr. Kyle put the paper down. "You made a comment, Miss Wade, about wanting good to come out of this evil. I can't guarantee that, but this is something that might help make a difference." He pointed to a small stack of papers on his desk. "I made copies if anyone wants one."

Several students raised their hands and, as the teacher passed the leaflets out, an idea began to simmer in Wendy's head. She wouldn't be going to college until fall. Maybe this might be the perfect thing to do. Her way of doing something right.

Chapter Fourteen

When Wendy woke Saturday morning, the sun was already streaming through her window, a sure indicator that she'd overslept. Whether she was tired or just needed the comfort of being bundled safely in her bed after Dr. King's assassination, she didn't know. Probably a bit of both or her mother would have knocked on her door earlier.

Throwing on some faded jeans and an oversized sweater, she made her way down the stairs to the smell of pancakes and maple syrup. Maybe she hadn't slept in that late after all if her mom was still cooking breakfast. Then she heard the sound of voices coming from the kitchen. She recognized Jo's and, a second later, Luke's. Wendy shook her head to clear it. With the horrible events taking place, she'd completely forgotten that Luke would be coming home for the college's Spring Break, which coincided with Easter weekend this year. Jo had probably mentioned it a dozen times recently. That at least explained the pancakes. They were Luke's favorite.

But Wendy was surprised when she entered the kitchen to see Mary Anne sitting at the table too.

"Where did you come from?"

Her sister arched one dark brow. "From Minneapolis, of course."

"Well, duh. I know that. I meant, why are you here?

You never said you were coming home for Easter."

"It was kind of a spur-of-the-moment thing," Mary Anne answered. "We just both felt like driving out. James dropped me a few minutes ago."

What Mary Anne probably wasn't saying was that they felt a need for the comforts of home too, after the TV news. Wendy studied her sister. She'd cut her hippie-long hair and wore it now in a smooth, chin-length pageboy. Gone, too, was the heavy eye makeup with ghost-white lips. Instead, she wore only a bit of mascara and a more natural pink lipstick.

Wendy plopped down in a chair. "So how long can you stay?"

"Just until Monday. I've got a new job and have to be back to work on Tuesday."

"Where are you working?" Luke asked, slicing into a pancake with his fork.

"At a bank. I'm a teller."

"Wow," Jo said, before turning her attention back to Luke and offering him butter. "That's pretty cool."

Wendy tried not to notice how lovey-dovey Jo was acting. Or how Luke kept smiling at her. They were acting mushy enough to make the butter melt without any help. Instead, she concentrated on her sister.

The job probably explained Mary Anne's new look. When she came back from San Francisco last year, she'd still been somewhat rebellious, even though she claimed the hippie movement wasn't what it was cracked up to be. She'd managed to graduate from high school, then moved to Minneapolis and gotten a job in a funky clothing store while James attended college.

"Is it fun handling all that money?" Wendy asked. "Like, do you pretend it's yours?"

Mary Anne shook her head. "Thinking like that could get me into trouble."

"We certainly don't want that," their mom said as she set a plate of more pancakes on the table. "Working as a bank teller is a very responsible position."

"It is," Mary Anne replied. "I have to balance to the penny every single day."

Wendy laughed as she helped herself to the pancakes. "You were terrible in math."

"It's *counting*, not algebra." Her sister shrugged. "I just have to be very careful that bills don't stick together and stuff like that."

"It's a good job." Luke took another pancake from the stack and doused it in syrup. "Banking is a stepping stone into the business world."

Mary Anne nodded. "I know. My supervisor said if I wanted a career, she'd mentor me. Eventually, I could become a loan officer or maybe even go higher in management."

Wendy nearly choked on the bite of pancake she'd just taken. Mary Anne wanted to have a career in management? Banking was one of the most conservative businesses there was, a polar opposite from her sister's wilder, more confrontational days. James must really, really, *really* have had an influence on her.

Wendy studied Mary Anne again. Even though she'd just seen her at Christmas, she seemed more mature...*content*, somehow. She and James didn't act all goo-goo over each other, but Wendy was beginning to suspect their relationship was getting more serious and involved.

She pasted a smile on her face so no one would notice how suddenly lonely she felt. Jo and Mary Anne had found their true loves, it seemed. Even the twins had long-term girlfriends, although she wasn't going to bet the family farm on those lasting once everyone went to college.

For now, she was the odd person out. Her relationship—if she could call it that—with Kevin was at a standstill. They were friends, sure, but he was friends with Bridget too. Not to mention all the girls that had suddenly taken an interest in him since he'd saved Tim and Tommy from the river. And, he didn't act as attentive as he had last year. The Valentine dance had been a fiasco and he hadn't asked her on a date, either. Of course, he didn't have a car nor could he get a job, because he needed a work visa. Still. Those were excuses. Weren't they?

She sighed inwardly, keeping the smile in place. Something needed to give soon to change the situation. She just didn't know what it would be.

****

"So are you and Wendy an item yet?" James asked as he and Kevin brushed down his horse late Saturday morning.

"Nae." Kevin hated admitting to it, but what was the alternative? In a small place like Middletown, James would hear all the gossip within an hour of leaving the farmhouse.

James peered over the mare's withers at him. "Why not? Don't tell me you've lost interest in her? Not after last year."

Kevin latched onto the last statement like a drowning man being tossed a lifeline. He could avoid the initial question by focusing on the last one. "I acted pretty stupid last year, followin' Wendy around like a puppy when she was interested in you."

James frowned. "I never thought she was interested in me."

"That's because *ye* were besotted with Mary Anne."

"That I was." James grinned and then sobered. "But it took me a while to get her attention. She thought she was in love with that Bob person." He leaned his forearms on the horse's back. "Is that the problem? Wendy likes someone else?"

"Nae." Kevin paused. "Aye. Maybe."

"That's real definitive."

"Och, I am nae sure. There's this guy that moved here from Minneapolis that she's real nice to."

One of James' eyebrows rose. "*Nice* to? How nice?"

"I...I can't really explain. He keeps to himself. Does nae mix with the rest of us. When we work on our group project, Wendy always compliments him."

"On the project? Or himself?"

Kevin shrugged. "Both." Most of the time, she asked Dwayne questions then agreed with his answers, but there were times when she complimented him on something he wore. Usually when he had something on that wasn't black.

"Does she flirt with him?"

"Nae. Not that I can tell."

James went back to finishing brushing the horse. "Then I don't think you have to be worried."

"But she doesn't flirt with me either." Kevin gave the mare a final pat on her neck and moved out of the stall.

James followed him. "So no dates?"

"Well, she asked me to the Valentine's dance. Girls were supposed to ask the guys."

"There you go, then. She does like you." James put the brushes up on a rack. "How did that go?"

"All right, I guess."

"You guess?"

"Another girl—Bridget, the girl from Ireland that I wrote ye about—asked me first."

"Oh." James made a sympathetic sound in his throat. "So you didn't take Wendy to the dance."

"Aye. I did. I took them both."

James stared at him. "Both?"

Kevin nodded. "I couldn't very well tell Bridget nae after I'd said aye."

"I agree." James knit his brows together. "But why did you say yes to Bridget in the first place?"

"There was little more than a week before the dance and Wendy hadn't asked, so I didn't think she was goin' to." Kevin shrugged again. "Besides, Bridget misses Ireland so she sees me as a friend from home."

"You're sure of that?"

"Aye. And I've told her she reminds me of my sister Mary. We're just friends."

"Okay. So the two of you agree you're friends. Does Wendy know how you feel about Bridget?"

"'Tis nae somethin' I can just blurt out, can I? Wendy's never asked."

James' mouth quirked. "You really don't think she'd *ask*, do you? If I'm learning anything about girls at all, it's they do *not* want to embarrass themselves by looking foolish."

Kevin grimaced. "I don't want to look foolish either. I pretty much got rejected once already."

"Last year," James said. "Things have changed. Besides, you don't have to declare undying love for

Wendy. Just let her know that Bridget is only a friend you talk to sometimes."

"Well…"

"Well, what?" James asked. "Is there more to this than you're telling me?"

"Nae. Aye. Maybe."

"You keep saying that. Just spit it out."

Kevin took a deep breath. "Bridget likes to cook. When I was sick, she brought over Irish food."

"So? She brought over something. Lots of people do that here."

"Well…" Kevin paused once more. "It was more than just once."

"Like how often?"

"Every couple of days. Then, when I got better, Mrs. Lambart decided she liked Irish cookin' and asked Bridget to keep comin' over. Wendy was there a couple of times when it happened."

"Ah. And Wendy got jealous?"

"She ran off both times before I could say anythin', so I don't know."

James grunted. "If Wendy left without saying anything, she was definitely jealous."

"How do ye know that?"

"Believe me. Both the Wade girls love to talk. And neither of them is timid, either. If Wendy didn't stick around, it was because she didn't want to take second place."

"But I wouldn't want her to take second place."

James patted him on the back. "You are telling the wrong person, laddie. You'd best tell Wendy."

It was Kevin's turn to stare. What if James was right? Then again, what if he was wrong? By the saints!

He *wanted* to tell Wendy she would always be first. But how was he to do it?

****

A very late spring snowstorm delayed the start of school after the Easter holiday, and by the time they returned to classes, not only had another riot broken out, this one in Washington, DC, but violence had occurred much closer to home.

A charred cross had been found in Lionel Jackson's front yard.

The entire student body seemed to be in the cafeteria, which wasn't that strange since everyone congregated there until the bell rang for first period, but the usual hum of conversation sounded more like a thundering waterfall when Wendy walked in on Wednesday morning. She turned to a freshman standing nearby. "What's going on?"

"You haven't heard?" the girl asked excitedly. "The KKK came to town Monday night."

"*What*?"

Either Wendy's incredulous tone of voice or the realization that she was speaking to a senior, made the frosh pause. Her tone was more subdued when she answered. "Well, no one actually *saw* anyone wearing a white hood, but someone tossed a burnt cross on the Jackson's yard."

Wendy stared at her. "Are you sure?"

The girl nodded. "My brother is in the seventh grade with Lysander Jackson. They're friends. Lysander called him, crying."

Wendy supposed she'd cry too if something like that had happened to her. She thanked the girl, who scudded off to find her friends, and then looked around for Lionel.

She didn't see him or his sister La Shonda, who was a junior. Maybe their parents had kept them home today. She just hoped they weren't in danger.

"I can't believe something like this has happened here in Middletown." She heard her voice shake as she joined Kevin, Bridget, Jo, and the twins at a table in the lunchroom.

"It kind of reminds me of what happened in Ireland last spring," Kevin said. "The Catholics up north formed the Northern Ireland Civil Rights Association to protest discrimination in hiring and housing."

Bridget nodded. "I remember that too. The Irish Catholics didn't trust the Special Constabulary in Ulster to be fair because they were Protestant."

"And there were offshoot groups," Kevin continued. "that would throw Molotov cocktails and stuff like that."

"Usually at night," Bridget added.

"I know when I lived in Brooklyn there were incidents, too, especially after the Equal Opportunity Employment thing went into effect." Jo turned to Kevin and Bridget. "Kind of like in Ireland, I guess."

"But Brooklyn and Belfast are big cities," Wendy said. "We're just a tiny town in the middle of farming country."

"I guess it just shows it can happen anywhere, just like Mr. Kyle mentioned in class," Tommy said. "Even here."

"But everyone has always gotten along," Wendy said. "We have different churches, but it doesn't matter which one you belong to. And almost everybody has a job. Nobody fights over that either. We've always accepted everyone."

"That's probably because your grandparents, your

great-grandparents, and even farther back, have always lived here. They settled the land," Jo said. "But in just the last three years since I came here, more people have moved in from other places."

"I guess it is different now, with the casino down the highway drawing crowds every weekend from the Twin Cities," Tommy said. "Maybe someone staying at one of the motels did it."

"But how would a stranger know where Lionel lived?" Wendy asked.

Tim looked thoughtful. "They might have seen one of the Jacksons around town—we are small, like you said. Maybe someone followed one of them."

"That's creepy," Wendy answered.

"What's creepy?" a different voice asked.

Wendy jumped and then turned in her seat to see Dwayne standing not far away. She felt a moment of embarrassment as she remembered he'd called on Saturday and she hadn't returned his call. With Mary Anne being home and then the snowstorm keeping James and her from going back until yesterday, she'd forgotten about the call. She'd have to apologize later.

"Someone threw a burnt cross on Lionel's lawn Monday night," she said. "We were just talking about who could have done it. Not knowing is kind of scary."

"I wouldn't worry about it." Dwayne shrugged. "It probably was a one-time thing and won't happen again."

Wendy frowned. "But the Jacksons were more than likely scared to death."

He gave her a long look as the bell rang. Whatever he might have said was lost in the bustle of chairs scraping the floor as students pushed them in at the tables and gathered books and jackets.

"Well, I hope Lionel is in Government today so we can talk," Wendy said as she pushed her chair in. "See you later."

"Later."

****

Later. Dwayne watched Wendy leave, in no hurry to get to class himself. Yes, *later*. She didn't return his phone call this weekend. He didn't like that one bit. He'd had big plans for them. Big plans that had to be put on hold. He didn't like anyone upsetting his plans. Not even her.

The tardy bell rang as The Hound came into the cafeteria to round up stragglers. Dwayne moved in the opposite direction. He didn't need any orders from that idiot either.

Then he smiled. At least, he'd been successful with one thing this weekend. None of the Jacksons were at school.

Chapter Fifteen

Lionel wasn't in last period Government. Wendy had hardly expected to see him since he hadn't been at lunch either, but she hoped he would be at school tomorrow. He needed to know he had friends.

"Today is a somber day," Mr. Kyle said as the bell rang to begin class, "but perhaps it gives us a chance to reflect, as well."

"What do you mean by that?" someone asked.

"It seems that Middletown is no longer immune from the effects of the Civil Rights movement."

"Nobody has rioted," Dwayne said. "No buildings looted or burned."

"No, but what happened to our small community might be far worse." The teacher paused. "Small towns have always been sanctuaries of sorts. It seems that era is gone."

That made Wendy think. "Kind of like in that book *Gone With The Wind*?"

"That could be used as an analogy," Mr. Kyle said. "The South that Scarlett O'Hara grew up in was forever changed by the Civil War."

"But that's a good thing, isn't it?" Mark asked. "I mean, slavery was abolished."

"Quite right," Mr. Kyle answered, "but I think Wendy was referring to the genteel lifestyle and culture that not only plantation owners had, but other

147

Southerners too."

Wendy nodded. "The book opens with a big lawn party. All the neighbors are at Tara and dressed up and having a good time. The weather is perfect. No one is worried about anything. They are enjoying life like they've always known it. Just like we do here in Middletown."

"But all that changed when the war came," one of the girls said.

"*Everything* changes when there's war," Mark answered. "Just look what Vietnam's done to us. Thousands of our soldiers have been wounded and thousands more won't be coming home."

"But does that mean the fights are nae worth it?" Kevin asked. "The colonists rebelled against England for the right to rule themselves. So did Ireland."

"In a way, it's kind of the same," Tommy said.

"Yeah," Tim added. "The South Vietnamese might not be slaves, but we're trying to keep them free from Communism."

"But Vietnam is half a world away, and they aren't Americans," Mark replied.

Dwayne turned to Mark. "You are right. We should take care of our own people."

"There! Someone who agrees with me!" Mark looked triumphant.

Wendy smiled at Dwayne. "I'm glad you said that. We all need to band together for Lionel when he gets back."

For a minute, Dwayne looked disconcerted. Then he shrugged. "He won't want our help."

"Why wouldn't he?" Tim asked. "He needs to know he has friends here."

Tommy nodded. "Probably whoever threw that burnt cross isn't even from here."

Dwayne smiled a little. "Probably not."

"But it still drives the point home," Mr. Kyle said. "Life in small towns, just like on the old Southern plantations, is changing. No longer can we sit quietly by and think violence only happens in big cities. Since the police don't know—yet—who did this, we have to be vigilant."

"Or vigilantes," one of the guys said.

"Violence isn't the answer, man." Mark gave him a disgusted look.

"Who would we fight, anyway, to get revenge for Lionel?" Another student asked. "We don't know who did it."

"And that is a matter for the police," Mr. Kyle said. "Hopefully, they will find the culprit soon and Middletown can hold onto its peace for a bit longer."

"It's a little bit like King Arthur's times, isn't it?" Bridget asked unexpectedly. When everyone turned to her, she flushed. "I mean, I always thought the legends were so sad. King Arthur had established peace and made good laws that his knights upheld. Then the Round Table came crashing down. Like in the movie… *"for one brief shining moment that was known as Camelot."* Is Middletown going to be like that?"

While her question brought on a surge of comments comparing the condition of medieval England to the present day, Wendy let herself withdraw into thought.

Was Middletown changing? Like Tara and Camelot, could it ever return to the simple, peaceful place it had been? Or was this just a start to the end of the road?

****

To Wendy's relief, Lionel was back in school the following Monday. She'd been worried when he'd been absent all week, but one of the teachers had said that the Jacksons needed time to reconcile what had happened. Lionel was tight-lipped and looked sullen, although she couldn't blame him for that. She'd probably feel the same—if not scared—if something that horrible had happened to her.

The police so far had no clues who might be responsible. The Jacksons lived on one of the busier streets near the highway, so any number of cars could have driven by that night. No one had seen or heard anything out of the ordinary, but it probably hadn't taken long to toss a cross that had already been burned somewhere else onto a lawn.

She smiled at Lionel as he walked past. "I'm glad you're back."

He gave her a grudging nod. "Thanks for checking on me."

He said the words so softly, she almost didn't hear him. She'd called over the weekend and his mother had said everyone was fine, but Wendy hadn't talked to Lionel. "I just wanted to be sure you were okay."

He nodded again and Dwayne gave her a sharp look, although he didn't say anything.

Mr. Kyle took roll call. "Instead of our usual Monday project work, I thought we might discuss a different kind of project this afternoon."

Wendy wondered if maybe the teacher didn't want to give the class too much leeway to talk today. In addition to the Washington, DC looting and burning, rioting had been rampant in Chicago, Baltimore and Cleveland and there were rumors that students at major universities were going to stage protests. Mr. Kyle probably thought it safer if they all stayed in their seats. If they were at their tables, everyone would want to discuss what had happened with Lionel's family.

"It's a project that I brought up a couple of weeks ago." Mr. Kyle pulled down a screen, turned on the overhead projector, and adjusted a transparency. "I thought it might be appropriate to talk more about Global Leadership Adventures, otherwise known as Teen Peace Corps."

"That's where we get to go to foreign lands, right?" a girl asked.

"Right."

"Hey, maybe I don't have to go to Canada then," Mark said. "I could pick and choose where to hang out."

Mr. Kyle gave him a stern look. "That's not its purpose. The idea is if young students spend some time in a developing country, they will gain an understanding for those cultures."

"It's kind of like the foreign exchange program," Kevin said, "except we spend a whole year in a school to learn about life there."

Bridget nodded. "And when I go back to Ireland, I can dispel some of the rumors about Americans as not true."

Dwayne lifted both brows. "What rumors?"

"Ah…well…just stuff." Bridget looked embarrassed. "Sometimes people have the wrong ideas."

"Precisely," Mr. Kyle said. "And that's what the GLA wants to help fix. It's just for a few weeks over the summer—not a whole year like the FEP—but it gives students an introduction to other countries and also a chance to help hands-on."

"So can I go to Paris?" a girl asked. "I'd love to see the latest fashions."

"Or London?" Another girl giggled. "Those British bands are so cool."

Mr. Kyle's smile looked a bit strained. "Paris is not a developing country. Neither is London. What this program wants to do is get you to understand and have tolerance for people in struggling countries."

"I guess that means Rome is out too," a boy said. "I wanted to see gladiators fight."

"Man, like that was a thousand years ago," Mark said.

"Actually, closer to fifteen hundred." Kevin shrugged when Mark scowled. "Part of Celtic history. The Romans invaded Britain."

"Well, no one is going to Rome unless it's on vacation." Mr. Kyle pointed to the list of countries on the transparency. "South America, India, Africa, Asia…"

"I get it now," a student said. "You think if we go to somewhere in Asia we'll understand the Vietnamese people better?"

"There is that hope."

Mark's chin jutted out. "It doesn't mean we should support the war over there, though."

"I'm not saying that," Mr. Kyle answered. "But the first step to stop the violence, both in this country and around the world, is to be tolerant of others."

Wendy glanced sideways at Lionel. Although nothing had been said about what had happened, or even Civil Rights, she was pretty sure the teacher meant to assure Lionel that there were still good people around.

She looked back at the list. She'd already decided the first time Mr. Kyle had mentioned the program that she'd like to do it. There were a lot of African countries listed. Perhaps that would be a place to start.

****

"I think the Global Leadership sounds like a good thing." Wendy glanced at Kevin as they waited for the bus after school. "It would be a chance to do something positive."

"I hadn't really thought about it like that, but ye're right," Kevin answered. "Everything on the news seems so negative all the time."

The bus lumbered up and everyone climbed on. Wendy managed to secure the spot beside Kevin and continued the conversation. "I think somewhere in Africa would be interesting. With so many problems going on with Civil Rights in America, I think it would be good to learn about black heritage."

"Kind of like gettin' to the heart of the matter?"

"Sort of, I guess," Wendy replied. "I don't think the program would send me anywhere really dangerous, but I'd like to go to Congo."

Kevin smiled. "Well, that is right in the middle of the continent. Ye can't get much more immersed than that."

Wendy nodded. "I'd like to see the animals, too. Imagine a lion in the savannah or an elephant on the veldt!"

"Just not up too close, though."

"I was thinking of a nice, safe truck."

"Aye, good! I'd hate to think of ye wanderin' about at the mercy of wild beasts."

Wendy gave him a covert look. Was he really concerned or just teasing? For just a moment she allowed herself to think of him coming to find her lost in the bush, the sun flashing off the silver of armor…she shook her head. Geez. Could she not get King Arthur's knights out of her imagination? Not only would heavy steel armor be hot, Kevin would probably be riding a zebra instead of a magnificent white horse. That thought made her giggle.

"What's so funny?"

She felt her face warm. "Nothing."

"Tell me anyway."

"Well…okay." She'd just leave out the part of knighthood. "I pictured you riding a zebra."

"I would nae mind tryin'."

Wendy stared at him. "You wouldn't!"

Kevin grinned. "I hear they're a wee bit cantankerous."

"Talk about being at the mercy—"

"Speaking of horse-like animals…" Jo leaned forward from her seat behind them. "Are we going to start practicing for the June horse show this Saturday?"

"I guess we'd better. Otherwise the other horse clubs will beat us." Wendy turned to Kevin. "You'll participate, won't you? They have events in both Eastern and Western saddle, along with jumps."

"Jumps? I don't know if James' horse is trained for those."

"He is," Jo said. "Tim and Tommy trained James— and the horse—last year."

Kevin raised an eyebrow. "Tim and Tommy?"

"Yeah, I know," Jo said. "It's hard to imagine them being serious about anything, but they did a good job."

"They spent time in England when they were sophomores," Wendy explained. "That's when they learned to jump. We're gradually getting more and more kids who want to do it, so it's turning into a real competition."

"Then count me in."

"Maybe you can show them a thing or two, since your dad trains horses too," Wendy said.

"Hey, we heard that!" Tommy said from the seat across from Jo.

Tim leaned forward to leer at Wendy. "Our cousin's deserting us for her—"

"I'm not deserting you, idiots," Wendy interrupted before Tim could finish his remark. She was positive he was going to say *boyfriend*. She would be totally mortified. Totally. Especially since she was sitting next to Kevin. She needed to change the subject fast before they launched into full teasing mode. "Maybe you two should concentrate on keeping your boiled eggs on your spoons this time. Carla and Susan beat both of you last year. They lasted all the way through the trot and the canter."

"That was just luck," Tim muttered.

"Maybe we were being chivalrous and *let* them win," Tommy countered. "It was their first year and all."

"So that's going to be your story when they win again this year?"

Tommy narrowed his eyes. "What makes you think they're going to win?"

Wendy shrugged. "Just sayin'."

"We're going to win *lots* of events this year," Tim said. "You wait and see."

"Not holding my breath," Wendy answered and then smiled as the twins started debating strategies between themselves. She had successfully diverted their teasing

At least, for now.

****

Jo grimaced as the first big plops of rain splashed onto the paddock fence Saturday morning. "Darn it. I just got all the jumps set up and now it starts to rain."

Wendy looked up at the sky. The heavy gray clouds didn't portend a casual shower, but more like an all-day soaker. Still, she didn't want to be the spoiler for Jo's plans to practice for the horse show. Her cousin was still as horse-crazy as she had been five years ago when she'd come here and learned to ride. "Maybe it will pass over."

More plops fell in faster succession. Jo shook her head. "I doubt it."

Hearing horses' hooves on the gravel yard road, Wendy pointed. "Looks like the twins and Kevin are more optimistic than we are."

Jo's gaze followed her gesture. "Looks like it, since they all have their Eastern saddles on."

Wendy looked past Tim and Tommy, who wore matching shirts and jodhpurs, to Kevin. Although he also used an English saddle, he'd worn comfortable jeans and a plaid flannel shirt that made his shoulders look really broad. The material, with its dark green and blues and thin lines of yellow running through it, set off his golden eyes and longish auburn hair. He looked every inch an Irish horseman.

A steady drizzle began as the guys dismounted, and Jo sighed. "I think you made the trip over for nothing."

"Not if Aunt Viv has cookies baked," Tim said as they led their horses inside the barn.

"And hot chocolate," Tommy added. "It's already feeling chilly."

Wendy laughed. "You're just using that as an excuse, but yes, Mom is doing her usual Saturday morning baking."

"That sounds great," Kevin said.

"Come on, then," Wendy answered. "I can make the chocolate."

Tim looked heavenward. "Don't poison us."

Since he was standing next to her, Wendy kicked his shin. "I've never poisoned you."

"No? Remember the time you tried to make eggnog?" Tommy asked. "We all almost got salmonella."

Geez. Did he have to bring up that in front of Kevin? "I didn't know Mom intended to throw those eggs away." She glared at Tommy. "Besides, that was three years ago. You're still alive."

Tim snickered. "Only because Aunt Viv thought it safer to keep you out of the kitchen."

She was going to *murder* her cousin. Bridget cooked delicious casseroles and scones. Kevin would think she couldn't even boil water. "Only for the holidays," she retorted. "She doesn't like anyone in the kitchen then."

Tommy raised a brow. "Didn't she put a 'keep out' sign on the door with your name on it?"

She was going to murder both of them. "It didn't have my name on it!"

"Stop bickering, you guys," Jo said. "I'm all for hot chocolate regardless of who makes it."

"I agree." Kevin said. "And I can't wait to taste those cookies."

Maybe she really should learn how to bake something, Wendy thought a short time later as they all sat around the kitchen table with a plateful of cookies that were disappearing rapidly while the rain drummed against the windows. Kevin had given her mother about a dozen compliments already.

Apparently, the twins noticed his solicitousness as well. "A guy could really get used to hanging around here, right?" Tommy asked with a mouthful of sugar cookie.

Tim picked up a chocolate chip one and looked askance at Kevin. "Yeah, Aunt Viv makes great cakes and pies too."

Oh, no. What were the twins up to now? Wendy eyed them suspiciously. That they were both looking back at her with innocent expressions did not bode well.

The phone rang just then, giving Wendy a reprieve.

Jo jumped up. "That will be Luke. I'll be back later."

"Our aunt cooks great meals too." Tommy moved the nearly empty plate toward Kevin after Jo had gone. "Luke practically lived here."

Oh, no.

"And Aunt Viv always insisted Mary Anne's dates come for dinner," Tim said helpfully. "Have you been invited yet?"

Oh, no, no, no. Her blasted cousins were trying to matchmake. From the uncomfortable expression on Kevin's face, he knew it too. If the way her face heated was any clue, she was probably as red as a tomato. It was a good thing her mother had left the kitchen or she'd probably invite Kevin to dinner right here and now.

"I'm sure Mrs. Lambart is a good cook too," Wendy said weakly.

"Not debating that," Tommy said before Kevin could answer. "It's just that Wendy doesn't have a date for Prom—"

"Prom isn't until the end of May." Wendy was pretty sure the color of her face had gone from tomato to beet. Lord, she didn't even want to think about Prom.

The Valentine dance had been a disaster. She didn't want a repeat.

"It's less than a month." Tim smirked. "Carla and Susan are already shopping for dresses."

"Good for them."

"You could shop with them…" Tim glanced at Kevin. "…if someone asked you to go to Prom."

Oh, please. Let the earth open and swallow me…

Tommy nodded to Kevin. "Aunt Viv would cook for you probably every night."

Never mind the earth opening. I'll just slide under the table and die quietly.

Unfortunately, that didn't happen. She remained upright in her chair. She wished she'd at least have the ability to faint, but that didn't happen either. Instead, Kevin squirmed in his chair and then cleared his throat.

"I've been wanting to ask you—"

"*No!*" Wendy pushed back from the table so hard she upset her chair when she stood. "I won't be a charity case!"

And with that, she ran from the room.

Chapter Sixteen

Had he offended the Fae? Or perhaps unwittingly insulted a leprechaun? Or maybe *an Diabhail* himself had a hand in his bad luck. Kevin could think of no logical reasons for the complete debacle that had occurred on Saturday. And he'd spent the whole weekend thinking about it.

It was nearly time for Monday's Government class. Mr. Lambart had dropped him off at school this morning because he'd been late—deliberately—in catching the bus and then he'd lingered outside school so long he was almost late for first period. He didn't go to the cafeteria for lunch. He had actually given a fleeting thought to skipping last period.

Coward that he was.

Or, at least, he felt like one. He had no clue what he could say to Wendy to make her feel better. She had fled to her room after the disaster. He could hardly have gone there. Tim and Tommy had tried to brush the whole thing off like it was some kind of joke. He'd found himself getting angry, so he'd left, nearly bumping into Jo as she came back from her phone call.

It wasn't that he didn't want to take Wendy to Prom. He *did*. But it was awkward when he didn't have a car. What girl wanted to have her mother or another adult drive them to the dance? Mrs. Lambart had solved that dilemma last Thursday by saying he could borrow her car, although he thought she was hoping he'd ask Bridget to go. Which might have been a problem except that Bridget had told him just last Friday after school that she didn't plan to go. He suspected she said that so he wouldn't feel obligated. He'd given her a hug for that. A *brotherly* hug.

And so, with his path clear, he'd been trying to figure out a way to ask Wendy. Had actually hoped to do that on Saturday.

But then Fate had intervened. Or the twins had. *B'fhearr leam gun robh thu ann an h-Irt!* He made himself think in English. He'd gladly send them to St. Kilda!

Kevin couldn't remember anything he'd botched so badly. Nor could he remember ever bumbling like he'd done when he'd choked out the invitation. By the saints! He'd have turned *himself* down.

Worse though, *much, much* worse, was that Wendy thought she was a charity case. That he'd asked her only because she didn't have a date and he'd been forced to be polite. Nothing could be farther from the truth, but how could he convince her of that?

Which is why he'd acted like a coward all day.

Kevin groaned as the bell rang to dismiss sixth period and move on to the next class…Government. He still didn't know what to do. And this was their project day. They'd be in groups working together. How should he act? Casual? A friendly "hi" as though nothing unusual had occurred on Saturday? Could he even pull that off?

He could hardly bring up the topic with the group there, but maybe he could ask to talk to Wendy after school. Then again, if she said no… Maybe he should just follow her out, then pull her aside. But…would he have time to explain before the bus came? And there'd be other kids around. Maybe even Tim and Tommy, blast them.

No. He needed to talk to her alone. Maybe the best thing to do would be to slip her a note, asking her to allow him a moment? That might work best. Maybe he could even make the question rhyme with something so it would sound almost like a poem. His sister Mary liked poems. Kevin hoped Wendy did too. He breathed a little sigh of relief at his decision and entered the classroom.

Wendy wasn't there.

He took his place and stared at her empty seat. It wasn't like her to be late. Had she been at school today? With all of his tactics trying to avoid her until now, had she not been there all day?

The tardy bell rang and Mr. Kyle took roll. As the students moved to their project tables, Kevin felt dark laughter bubbling in his throat.

It seemed the Fae or *an Daibhail*—the devil himself—weren't quite through with him yet.

****

By noon, Wendy was restless. She'd tossed and turned in bed all morning, bored to tears. But here she would have to stay, after telling her mother that she'd thrown up this morning and was sure she was coming down with something. It hadn't been a total lie. She *had* felt nauseous. And she probably *would* have been sick if she'd had to go to school and face Kevin today.

It wasn't like her to be a coward, but she just couldn't face him. Not yet.

Wendy threw back the covers, then pulled them up again. Her mother was already suspicious. If she came in to find Wendy curled up in the window seat reading a book, she'd have her at school before lunch. Before *Government* class.

She knew she'd have to go to school tomorrow. With no fever, her mother wouldn't let her stay home another day, but at least on Tuesday they had a regular class with Mr. Kyle lecturing. If she slipped in at the last minute, she could just take her seat and not have to talk to Kevin.

Or her dim-brained cousins.

Just thinking about what they did Saturday made her face heat. Maybe if she stayed mad at them, her mother would mistake her heightened color for a fever? Even as she contemplated it, she knew it wouldn't work.

But that didn't mean she wouldn't get revenge. She would. Not only had they made her sound like some pathetic wallflower whom no one would ask to Prom, they'd also backed Kevin into a proverbial corner where he felt forced to ask her to go with him. She hadn't missed the panicked look on his face or the way he could hardly get the words out.

Her mortification was complete.

What was she going to do?

Wendy punched the pillow and then fell back on it to stare at the ceiling. Her silly crush on James last year had never felt so agonizing, even after she finally figured out he liked Mary Anne. And last year, she and Kevin had been friends. They'd been able to laugh and talk and get along just fine. Why couldn't they do that now?

"Why?" she asked the ceiling. "Why can't things work out?"

"They usually do."

For a moment, Wendy wondered if maybe she *was*

feverish. The ceiling had answered her? Then she became aware that her mother was standing in the doorway.

She stepped inside with a cup of hot tea laced with honey and set it down on the nightstand. "What do you want to work out?"

This time when Wendy felt her face warm, she was glad. Maybe her mother would really buy into her being sick. She propped herself against the headboard and picked up the tea cup to take a sip, even though she didn't care much for the taste. "Thanks for bringing this."

"You're welcome." Her mother sat on the edge of the bed. "Now tell me what you want to work out."

Wendy forced another sip. Once her mom decided to pursue a question, there would be no stopping her until it was answered. Thankfully, she had been out of the kitchen when Tim and Tommy sprang their attack on Kevin. Jo said everyone left soon afterwards, so her mother wasn't aware of the disaster that had taken place.

"Just thinking about Saturday. We couldn't practice for the horse show because of the rain." At least, that wasn't a lie. *And*, if they had been able to practice, the twins wouldn't have had the chance to totally ruin her life.

"The horse show isn't until June. You'll have plenty of time to practice." Her mother gave her a thoughtful look. "Are you sure there isn't something else bothering you?"

"Nope. Nothing."

Her expression turned skeptical. "It seemed strange the boys left so suddenly Saturday."

Darn it. Was her mom not going to let this go? Wendy shrugged. "I guess there was no reason to stay.

They ran out of food."

Her mother raised an eyebrow. "There were several cookies left on the plate. I've never known the twins to leave even a crumb."

Blast it. Why couldn't they have finished those cookies? They usually gobbled up every sweet in sight. Even when they weren't present, they were getting her in trouble. "I don't know. I had…a tummy ache, so I left them in the kitchen." That was partially true. "I guess I was coming down with something even earlier."

Her other eyebrow rose. "I thought you said you were getting a cold."

"Well, yes…I…" Wendy floundered for words. She was *so* going to get revenge at the twins for making her dig a deeper hole. "Maybe it's the flu."

"Um. It's nearly May. Flu season's over." Her mother sighed and rose to leave. "If you want to talk about whatever it is, I'll be here."

"It's nothing." Wendy watched her mother leave, hating that she was keeping secrets. But this was something she was going to have to work out herself.

She drew her knees up and folded her arms around them. She could—*would*—tell Kevin that he needn't feel obligated to escort her to Prom. She wasn't going to be a charity case. She'd meant that. If Kevin had really wanted to go to Prom with her, he'd have asked on his own. Besides, she'd *seen* him hug Bridget last Friday after school. More than likely, she was the one he really wanted to ask. Wendy wiped back tears. In the battle for Kevin's heart, she'd lost.

But she had a dilemma on her hands. If she said she was just going to stay home, Kevin would feel guilty. While he might be Bridget's knight in shining armor and not *hers*, she knew he would try to be gallant and do the right thing. Wendy remembered the Valentine's dance all too well. She definitely did not want a repeat of that.

She couldn't even use the excuse that Jo wouldn't be going, since Luke planned to come down from St. Cloud for that weekend. For a moment, she considered having Jo ask him to bring a friend along to be her date. Then she rolled her eyes. Like some college guy would want a blind date to take a high school girl to her Prom. Fat chance.

But… Wendy hugged her knees harder. If she *had* an actual date—maybe one of the guys she'd known since kindergarten who would be going stag?—then Kevin would be off the hook. He wouldn't feel obligated to take her. She really, really, *really* did not want to be a charity case.

That posed another problem. Wendy sighed. All the guys she'd grown up with either had girlfriends or she just didn't find them interesting. She would be bored out of her tree having to put up with one of them, even a friend, for an entire evening.

But her mother thought Senior Prom was a big deal. She might suggest that Wendy join the other girls who would be going alone. She couldn't think of a fate worse than standing around in a formal watching happy couples dance. Especially one happy couple.

She definitely needed a date. Not anyone who was looking for a relationship or anything. Just someone to fill in for that one evening. But whom? Everybody she knew…

Wendy paused in her thinking as an idea sprang forward. Maybe someone not from here. Maybe someone who would understand and be willing to get out of his shell a bit for the evening.

Dwayne.

Prom might just be what he needed to make him feel a part of Middletown. She would ask him first thing tomorrow.

Chapter Seventeen

"You did what?" Jo set down her lunch tray and stared at Wendy as though she'd lost her mind.

"I asked Dwayne to the Prom."

"I heard what you said," Jo replied. "But I don't understand why you'd do something so dumb."

"Really dumb." Tommy grimaced. "After we got it all set up for you with Kevin—"

"That's just it!" Wendy put her sandwich down before she threw it at her cousins. "Thanks to your meddling—"

"We didn't *meddle.*" Tim shook his head. "We *helped.*"

"Some help! You made Kevin feel guilty."

"Why would he feel guilty?" Tommy asked.

"Because you made me sound like some poor misfit who couldn't get a date."

Tim shrugged. "Well, you didn't have a date."

"Beside the point," Wendy huffed.

"Anyway, you wanted to go with Kevin," Tommy added, "and he asked you, so why did you do something so stupid?"

"It wasn't stupid." Wendy glared at both of them. "If I didn't have a date, Kevin would feel *obligated* to take me—"

"Trust me." Tommy smirked at her. "He wouldn't mind feeling *obligated.*"

"I don't want him feeling sorry for me!"

"You think Kevin feels sorry for you?" Tim laughed out loud. "You sure are dense."

"Gee, thanks," Wendy said sarcastically. "Now I'm not only a misfit, I'm *dense*."

"Well, you *are*. You asked Dwayne Bernard to the dance."

"Nobody even likes him."

Wendy gave an exasperated sigh. "That's *why* I asked him. He feels like nobody likes him."

"He's right," Tommy said.

Tim nodded. "Because he's conceited."

"He's just introverted," Wendy replied.

Tim shrugged again. "Well, it's your funeral."

"Hope you don't mind seeing Kevin with another date." Tommy looked around the cafeteria. "About half the girls here would say yes in a second."

"Okay, stop it, you two." Jo intervened. "I don't agree with Wendy's choice, but I get that she doesn't want to be pitied. You guys forced Kevin into asking."

Wendy knew Jo said that to be loyal, but she also had just pointed out that Wendy was *right*. Kevin hadn't had any choice unless he wanted to be rude, and he would never do that. He really did act a lot like a gallant knight. But what she had forgotten, until last night, was that knights were *supposed* to rescue any lady in distress. They even had a code of chivalry that said so. So it didn't really matter if said knight—or Kevin, in this case— thought she was special or not.

She felt tears welling up and pushed back her chair to stand. She wasn't going to add to the twins humiliating her by crying in front of them. She had made the right decision.

What was that adage about if you loved something, to set it free…? Well, she had. Kevin wasn't obligated anymore.

But somehow, it didn't make her feel any better.

****

Bridget was waiting for him as Kevin made his way back into the main building from shop class later that afternoon.

"I'm sorry," she said.

He didn't bother to pretend he didn't know what she meant. He'd barely gotten inside the cafeteria this morning when Dwayne had sauntered over to inform him that Wendy was his date for Prom.

At first, Kevin hadn't believed him. Why would Wendy do something like that? He knew she was upset with the way he'd handled things—or not handled them—on Saturday, but she hadn't given him a chance to explain. Something akin to a horse's kick hit him in the stomach. Maybe she didn't want an explanation.

Did she really want to date the guy? He'd thought she was just being nice when they worked on their Government project, but maybe he had it all wrong. She hadn't paid all that much attention to him last year because she had a crush on James. But this year she had acted like she really liked him. At least, he thought she had. But maybe his brain was thick as a cement block. He tightened his jaw.

"No need to be sorry."

"Aye, and if ye think I'll be believin' that, ye insult me." Bridget lapsed into her natural brogue, a sure sign she was upset.

Kevin glanced at her. "Wendy made her choice, didn't she? It doesn't matter."

"Aye, but it does." She pushed her hair back. "I am just nae sure which of ye is the bigger fool."

Kevin stopped. "Why would ye think *me* a fool?"

"For nae fighting for her."

His brogue came out as well. "They doona allow fightin' at school. I'd be expelled."

Bridget looked heavenward. "Ye ken full well I dinna mean *physical* fighting. Doona be a dolt."

Kevin frowned. "Dolt?"

"Aye. Dolt. 'Tis as plain as your nose that she cares for ye."

"Then why did she turn me down when I asked her?"

Bridget gave him a look that said, plainly, he had limited thinking capacities. "From what I could glean from Jo, Wendy thinks ye dinna mean it because the twins forced ye to ask."

"Nae true. I meant to ask—"

"Meant to?" Bridget shook her head. "'Tis nae what a lass wants to hear."

"Well, there is naught I can do about it now." Kevin started walking, but Bridget put her hand on his arm and he stopped once more. "What? We're going to be late for class."

"Just one more question. Do ye care for her as much as I think ye do?"

Kevin's face heated. "I doona want to talk about it."

"Ye just answered my question." Bridget smiled. "I've a feelin' things will work out for ye."

He grimaced. "Unless ye have faerie blood, I'll nae put much faith in that."

Bridget widened her smile. "I have nae faerie blood, but who's to say the Fae are nae here? There's magic everywhere, if ye ken where to look."

Kevin shook his head as the tardy bell began to ring. "Come on. Hurry."

They made it inside the door just as the bell stopped. Mr. Kyle frowned at them as they took their seats. Kevin didn't look up. At least, being almost tardy meant he didn't have to say anything to Wendy just yet.

If there were faeries about, he hoped they were in a good mood and had a mind to help.

****

Wendy watched as Kevin and Bridget came in the door together, both of them a bit breathless. What had they been doing? Had Kevin given her another hug in the hall? Or maybe even a kiss? Was that why they were almost late? Middletown High School had a strict policy against public displays of affection, as The Hound was always happy to remind any students lingering in the halls. But maybe they had been outside—their cheeks were both pink—away from the assistant principal's prying eyes.

She tried to squelch her jealousy. She'd reminded herself a zillion times today that Kevin would never be her boyfriend. How long was it going to take before she believed herself?

Dwayne passed her a note, which she quickly hid under her book as she felt her face turn red. Mr. Kyle didn't like notes being passed in class. She would die of total embarrassment if he confiscated it. Looking up nonchalantly, she caught Kevin watching her. He looked quickly away, but she knew he'd seen the note being passed.

It was just a silly note, although it was the third one today. Dwayne had slipped one to her this morning in the cafeteria and she'd found another one stuck in her locker at noon. The first two had said something to the effect of showing her a really good time, so she assumed this one said the same.

She frowned slightly as she opened her book and pretended to read the pages assigned on the chalkboard. Why was Dwayne passing her these notes anyway? It wasn't like they were *dating*.

At least she hoped he didn't think that. She thought she'd made it quite clear that she was only asking for a favor so she wouldn't have to go with someone else whom "she'd heard" was going to ask her. He had laughed and said he understood. She had even thanked him for being a *friend* and bailing her out.

They were only friends. She didn't really care if she had a good time or not at Prom. Without Kevin as her date, it was simply an evening to get through.

And Kevin was *not* her date. He had probably already asked Bridget. For the zillionth-and-one time she reminded herself that he had no interest in being her boyfriend.

And neither was Dwayne. For sure.

****

Kevin hadn't meant to watch Wendy. He'd intended not even to look at her as class started. But what he'd intended to do wasn't what he'd done, so he'd seen her take the note that Dwayne had passed to her. *And* he had seen Wendy blush when she accepted it.

He opened his book with more force than was necessary, causing it to bang on the desk, which drew a startled look from Bridget seated across the row. He grimaced. She might believe in magic, but if the Fae were involved, they were sending a very clear message.

Wendy was perfectly happy that Dwayne Bernard was taking her to the Prom.

"Ye look as fierce as a troll guardin' its bridge," Bridget whispered.

"I am nae a troll!"

"I dinnae say that, did I?" She grinned. "Wendy might think ye are jealous."

Mr. Kyle cleared his throat. "If we are all ready to begin class?"

"Aye, sir. Sorry." Kevin forced a neutral expression. He certainly didn't want Wendy to think he was jealous or that the note mattered.

"Perhaps a bit of delay in starting won't matter," the teacher said, "considering we just keep getting negative news these days. As you all have probably heard, another riot broke out, this time at Columbia University."

"That's a big time Ivy Leaguer," someone said.

"You wouldn't think the rich boys would care about the common people," Mark muttered.

"Well, this protest is unusual in that it's twofold," Mr. Kyle replied. "The students are angry over institutional apparatus supporting the Vietnam war, and they're upset over a proposed segregated gym to be built in Morningside Park."

"So it's both anti-war and pro-Civil Rights?" Wendy asked.

"Exactly." Mr. Kyle looked at Mark. "Those students feel just as strongly as you do about the war."

Mark looked a little bit embarrassed. "I guess not all rich kids are bad."

"But you have a point," Lionel said. "Most rich kids don't care about us regular folk. *Especially* if you're black."

"Sounds like you have a chip on your shoulder," Dwayne remarked.

"Wouldn't you?" Lionel shot back. "Someone left a burnt cross on our lawn."

"End of conversation," Mr, Kyle intervened. "Today's discussion is going to be about what we can do to work for equality for everyone."

Kevin let his thoughts stray as the teacher began his lecture. He didn't know what Wendy saw in Dwayne. The guy acted like a real jerk sometimes, and Kevin didn't think it was jealousy rearing its head for him to think that.

But even now, she was looking at Dwayne. Kevin couldn't make out her feelings since she was neither smiling nor frowning, just watching. He sighed. In spite of Bridget trying to be encouraging, it really didn't matter since Wendy had made her decision. All he could do was pretend he didn't care by acting as if nothing was wrong.

He'd planned to reveal his little secret—that he'd applied for the Global Leadership Adventures so he could join Wendy this summer—at Prom. Now that wouldn't happen. His secret would stay just that.

Summer looked long and empty.

Chapter Eighteen

She had made one really dumb, stupid, idiotic, *big* mistake...the worst that Wendy could remember in her entire life. It topped her silly crush on James, or when she had tried to scare Jo at the river cabin by leaving her alone and pretending to be a wolf howling, or even the time she'd nearly poisoned her cousins with eggnog. None of that came close to what she'd done.

"Inviting Dwayne Bernard to Prom was the worst," she muttered to Jupiter as she led him out of his stall. The horse dipped his head as if in agreement. "Gee, thanks for making me feel better."

The gelding nodded his head again, this time nudging his muzzle into her shoulder, and she realized he was looking for his apple slice. The look in his large, limpid eyes was reproachful, though, and she wasn't entirely sure it was because she hadn't brought his treat. He probably thought her as much a fool as she did.

"Here." Jo handed her a couple of extra apple slices. "You forgot this earlier."

'Thanks." Wendy put them in her palm and held her hand out. Jupiter lipped both, crunching noisily, but the disparaging look in his eye didn't change. So, her horse did think she was a total nincompoop.

"I'm glad the sun finally came out and the rains stopped before the weekend." Jo led Silver toward the paddock and looked at the sky. "We finally have some decent weather to practice for the horse show."

"I guess." For over ten days they had gotten soaked. Heavy gray clouds scudding across a dark sky and cold, pelting, all-day rains had fit Wendy's mood perfectly. She'd even used the weather as an excuse when her mother questioned why she was so grumpy.

Jo pointed. "Here come the twins."

Wendy didn't have to turn to know Kevin wasn't with them. She shouldn't be surprised. For the past two weeks at school, he had been aloof. Polite, but only speaking to her when she directly asked a question. When they'd worked on their Government project, he'd partnered himself with Bridget, leaving her with Dwayne.

The worst thing was that she couldn't blame Kevin. She still shuddered at the expression on Kevin's face when Dwayne had announced that *she* had asked *him* to the blasted dance. If Kevin had been politely aloof before, he'd become coldly formal.

What she had thought would be the perfect solution to not having Kevin feel obligated to take her had turned into the perfect nightmare. And it was still two more weeks until that awful night would be over.

Dwayne only made the situation worse by continuing to send notes. She'd asked him to stop doing that during class because she didn't want teachers picking them up, but that hadn't kept him from sticking them in the slot of her locker. Unfortunately, Kevin's locker was near hers, and those bits of paper stuck out like a banner waving in the wind. She felt like she was sinking deeper and deeper into one of those infamous, mud-sucking bogs found in Ireland. Kevin had told her about them.

She certainly couldn't expect that almost-knight in shining armor to save her, either. Said knight hardly glanced her way these days. The only tiny—and she meant *tiny-miniscule-microscopic*—consolation she had was that Bridget said she'd told Kevin she wasn't going to the Prom.

Why Bridget would have refused him was beyond Wendy's understanding, but it made her feel even more remorse over her stupid, impulsive decision to ask Dwayne. Of course, that didn't mean Kevin hadn't asked someone else or someone hadn't asked *him*. Plenty of girls still talked about his rescuing the twins from the river, but she hadn't *heard* anything. Yet.

"Unless you want Tim and Tommy nagging you again, you'd better lose that sour face." Jo opened the paddock gate and gave Wendy a sympathetic look. "I don't think you need to feel any worse than you already do."

Wendy nodded, knowing her cousin was right. She'd spend the better part of the past two weeks alternating between crying in one of their bedrooms at night or ranting at herself for being a complete dope. Neither had helped very much, but at least she'd been able to put on a stoic face at school, thereby preventing the twins from hassling her.

She managed to paste on a semblance of a smile by the time they reached the paddock. Tim looked around.

"Kevin's not here?"

Of course, he wasn't here. Tim didn't need glasses to see that. But before Wendy could retort, Jo answered.

"I think he said yesterday he needed to help Mr. Lambart with something."

Tommy exchanged a doubtful look with Tim. "Are

you sure? He didn't say anything to us."

"It probably wasn't a big deal," Jo said.

Obviously unconvinced, Tim looked down at Wendy. "Did he say anything to you?

"Nope." Wendy swung up into the saddle, her lips nearly numb from having to keep the smile in place. "I didn't wait around after school yesterday."

That much was true, but Kevin didn't wait around either. He'd walked off in the direction of Mr. Lambart's office—like he'd done the past two weeks—and hadn't taken the bus home. Just like he hadn't done the past two weeks either.

Bridget had mentioned that he'd started working for Mr. Lambart after school, but Wendy wasn't sure that was true. Or maybe it was because he wanted to earn some money to spend on his Prom date, whoever she was.

"He really needs to be here to practice," Tommy said.

"Maybe we should call him?" Tim asked.

Wendy's mouth was really hurting now. Too bad she'd never enrolled in drama class. She just hoped she sounded convincing. "He's used to riding English saddle. We're not, so I suggest we get going."

Not waiting for their answer, she reined Jupiter around and headed for the first jump. She just wished her horse could soar into the sky and fly away.

****

All thoughts of her idiocy and Kevin's change in behavior disappeared by Monday. Someone had thrown another burnt cross on the Jacksons' front lawn sometime Sunday night. It was the headline for the local news on the radio this morning.

The cafeteria was quiet when Wendy walked in, reminding her of the other time this same, horrible thing had happened. She spotted the twins with Bridget and Kevin and made her way toward them. Now was not the time to worry whether Kevin wanted to talk to her or not.

"I can't believe it's happened *again*," she said as she and Jo sat down by the others.

Tommy nodded. "It pretty much zeroes out the theory that some stranger staying at a motel followed one of the Jacksons home last time."

"I guess you're right." Wendy felt a sudden sense of shame. "But people in Middletown don't act like this."

"Well, we *are* only a few miles from the casino," Tim said. "There are people from the Twin Cities who work there and rent apartments."

"Livin' in a big city makes it easy to be prejudiced and discriminate. Belfast is an example." Kevin shrugged when everyone turned to him. "'Tis a lot easier to dislike someone ye do nae know personally."

"But that's just it," Wendy said. "Everyone knows everyone in Middletown, and we've always welcomed strangers."

"Well, maybe before." Jo looked thoughtful. "But in the three years I've lived here, besides the casino, a manufacturing company has opened up down the road, as well as a water distillation plant in the other direction. That's several hundred people that are new to the area, even if they don't all live in Middletown."

Tommy frowned. "But a bunch of them do."

"Yeah," Tim agreed, "we must have added a couple dozen students just to the high school in the last three years."

"Aye," Bridget said. "Middletown High School had

enough students to qualify as a host to the foreign exchange program. 'Tis why Kevin and I are here."

Wendy tried to ignore the "Kevin and I" part. It sounded like he and Bridget were a couple. Even if they weren't going to Prom together, it was obvious they had some sort of special bond. One that Kevin didn't share with Wendy.

Jo gave her a poke, bringing her back to the present. More than likely, her cousin knew exactly where her rapidly spiraling negative thoughts were going. She felt another wave of shame wash over her for being so self-centered at a time like this.

"When Mr. Hoffman drove me to school this morning, we saw several police cars by the Jacksons' place," Bridget said. "Mr. Hoffman said two of them were state troopers."

"That makes sense, I guess," Tim said, "since Lionel lives right off a state highway."

"Another car was unmarked," Bridget replied, "and two men wearing suits were talking to the other police."

Tommy whistled. "It sounds like they called the FBI!"

Wendy widened her eyes. "That was really quick, if they did."

"In Brooklyn it only took minutes for all kinds of police to converge on a scene," Jo replied. "Minneapolis is only a couple of hours away. They probably drove over as soon as they got the call."

"I wonder if anyone saw anything this time."

"The guy on the radio said someone saw a dark green sedan driving away from that street and speeding out of town," Tommy said, "but it was gone long before the cops got there."

"Maybe this time they'll catch whoever did it," Kevin said.

"But wasn't the car seen leaving town?" Bridget asked.

"Doesn't mean it won't come back," Wendy said. "This is the second time this has happened. It can't be a coincidence."

Tim nodded. "I sure hope they catch the jerk. The sooner, the better."

"Before whoever the bum is does something more violent," Tommy added.

Wendy couldn't have agreed more. Whoever was doing this was ruining the Middletown she'd always known. And she didn't like the change one bit.

****

Wendy looked over at Lionel the next day in Government class. Since he was on an alternate schedule, she hadn't seen him until now. He sat tight-lipped and still, his face as hard as though he'd been chiseled from one of the local granite quarries.

She'd tried to tell him how sorry she was, but he'd just given her a jerky nod and not answered. She supposed she couldn't blame him. She had no idea how she'd react if something so hateful had been done to her.

Thankfully, this wasn't project day and Mr. Kyle kept his lecture on the effects of the election process that was heating up. Talking about whether Richard Nixon would win the Republican primary and Robert Kennedy the Democratic one kept the attention off Lionel and what had transpired.

The class ended with Mr. Kyle reminding the students that whichever candidate won, we had to come together as a country. And, he emphasized, getting to know everyone in a social setting was an easy way to develop that kind of unity.

Wendy wondered if he wasn't really referring to students uniting around Lionel.

"That kind of sounded like a 'love your enemies' sermon," Tommy said as they all walked out of the building after school.

"It's not a bad idea," Wendy said.

"Why would you care about your enemies?" Dwayne asked.

Wendy hadn't noticed that he'd followed her out, but she shouldn't have been surprised. The notes had stopped, but he seemed to be close every time she turned around. At least Prom was less than two weeks away and then they could go their separate ways.

"Ye haven't heard about 'keepin' your friends close, but your enemies closer'?" Kevin asked.

Dwayne gave him a level look. "Are you saying you and I are best buddies, then?"

Kevin returned the look. "I'm sayin' 'tis a wise thing to do."

"Okay," Wendy intervened before the situation escalated. "I think Mr. Kyle meant if we get to know each other in a social setting, we will see a person differently."

"Fat chance," Dwayne said.

Tommy cut in before Kevin could answer. "I'm all for social activities." He poked Tim. "How about you?"

Tim grinned. "Absolutely. Especially if those activities involve girls."

Wendy almost rolled her eyes at them, but at least they'd diverted a possible fight. "Like what kind of activities?" She knew it was a stupid question and one she'd probably regret asking, but if it kept the conversation light, then it would be worth the typical twins' answer.

"*Fun* activities," Tommy smirked.

Tim smirked too. "With *girls*."

She did roll her eyes at them then. "You two are *so* intelligent."

Tommy's smirk widened into a grin. "We try not to let it show."

"Don't worry," Wendy answered. "It doesn't."

"Geez, cuz. Cut us a little slack here," Tim said. "After all, not many guys would think of taking their girls to a cozy, *private* getaway in a cave."

"That's *original*," Tommy added for emphasis.

"Are you talkin' about the cave down by the river?" Kevin asked.

Wendy posed a second question. "The one that's probably damp and smelly, not to mention dirty?"

"Yes," Tim said to Kevin and turned to Wendy. "It's not damp or smelly or dirty. Not any more, anyway."

"Yeah, we cleaned it up. We put plates and stuff in there. Even candles to make it romantic."

"And lots of blankets to…sit on."

"Which are probably gathering mold," Wendy said.

"Now you're getting close to insulting us," Tommy said. "We put them in plastic sacks."

Wendy shook her head. "Mice will eat holes through those."

Tim smirked again. "We *double*-bagged them."

"Anyway, we're taking Carla and Susan up there soon."

"Hope they like bugs," Wendy said.

Tommy made a dramatic flourish with his arms. "Then we will act chivalrous and save our damsels from such danger."

Not to be outdone, Tim bowed low. "You aren't the only girl looking for a knight in shining armor, cuz."

Wendy felt her face grow warm. Why did they have to bring that up in front of Kevin? Would he think she'd cast him in that role? Not that she hadn't…she had. At least in her mind. She should never have let the twins know how much she liked the Camelot movie. Even worse, Kevin was watching her curiously.

"Is that what you want, Wendy?" he asked.

Oh, Lord…

"I've got it covered, O'Keefe," Dwayne said.

Kevin gave him an even look. "I wasn't talkin' to you."

Oh, Lord…

"But you were talking to *my* date for Prom."

Kevin stiffened and then he inclined his head. "So I was."

He abruptly turned and walked away.

Chapter Nineteen

How stupid could he be? Kevin chastised himself as walked in the direction of Mr. Lambart's office. He should have known better than to linger after class to talk to Wendy, especially when Dwayne Bernard hovered like a hawk. *Droch sgeul ort!* How he wished he could dig up some dirt on that guy.

Was Wendy really looking forward to going to Prom with him? Her face had turned red when Bernard reminded everyone she was his date, but was that from embarrassment or anticipation?

Tim and Tommy had teased her about wanting a knight in shining armor. He sure was no knight, but he didn't think Dwayne qualified as one either. Kevin grimaced as he reached Mr. Lambart's office. Bridget had told him to fight for Wendy. How could he when he didn't even know if she *wanted* him to?

"What's got you upset?" Janice, the matronly secretary-receptionist, asked as he walked in. "You look like someone's forced you to drink sour milk."

That thought made his stomach churn, not that it hadn't already been knotted up. Kevin loosened his shoulders to force himself to relax. "Just school stuff."

"Um." She raised a silvery brow. "Like girl stuff?"

"Nae." He grimaced again. "Nothin' I can't work out. I better get to work filin' the papers I didn't get to yesterday."

"I already did that."

"But that's part of what Mr. Lambart is payin' me to do so ye can attend to more important stuff."

Janice shrugged. "It's been a slow day. Anyway, Mr. Lambart had to go to an unexpected meeting this afternoon, so I didn't have to take dictation."

"Oh. Then…there's nothin' for me to do today?"

"I didn't say that." She smiled. "Maybe we should have a little chat."

Kevin shifted uncomfortably. "Chat" meant "talk" as in someone was going to tell him something he probably didn't want to hear. He'd already had one "chat" today. "I really don't have time."

"Of course you do. You're supposed to be working here for the next two hours." Janice motioned to an armchair nearby. "Go ahead and have a seat."

Since she was about the same age as his mother, he didn't want to argue with her. Tentatively, he sat.

She smiled at him. "Don't look so nervous. I'm not going to poke my nose into your business. At least, not too much."

"My business?"

"Well, actually Wendy Wade's business, more than yours."

That got his full attention. "What do you mean?"

"Middletown is small. I've known the Wades for forty-plus years. Such a tragedy when Vivian lost her husband. Then Mary Anne running away to San Francisco…" Janice tsked. "Of course, I'm glad Mr. Lambart's son went after her and brought her home—"

"Excuse me, ma'am." Kevin didn't really want to gossip about Wendy's family, and he knew, even in the short time he'd been working here, that once Janice got started, she'd go on like a maelstrom threatening to sink ships. "I don't think I'm part of whatever Wendy's business may be."

"Ah! But you're wrong there." Janice gave him a sly look. "You like her, don't you?"

Kevin tried not to squirm in his chair. "Well…sure. She's…nice."

"Psshh! That's not the word we used when I was young." Janice shook her head. "But I won't push you, since everyone knows it's true anyway."

He closed his eyes momentarily, wondering if he suddenly started praying, he could disappear. Was he really so transparent that the whole town knew?

"No need to be embarrassed," Janice went on. "Everybody is rooting for you."

He squeezed his eyes shut again. Sweet Mary and all the saints! The whole town *did* know! He silently pleaded for a crack in the floor to open, but nothing happened. Evidently, neither a Deity nor the Fae were going to help him. Kevin slowly opened his eyes to find Janice smiling at him.

"There now. Things aren't so bad."

No. They'd just gone from worse to *worst*. "I don't know what ye mean."

"Let me simply say it, then." Janice nodded, as if reconfirming something to herself. "That Bernard boy isn't good for her."

Kevin wasn't sure if he'd heard right. "Dwayne Bernard?"

"That's the one."

Well. Maybe things were a little bit better than worse or *worst*. "I won't argue that."

"Of course you won't." She straightened in her

chair. "The boy is from Minneapolis. City boys aren't brought up like those here."

That might be true, but Kevin felt a twinge of conscience about placing blame. Not that he wanted to defend Dwayne. "He's just...different."

"You have that right. And not in a good way."

Kevin's ears perked up. The secretary sounded like she knew something she wasn't telling. He could practically hear his own mother admonishing him not to encourage her, but if it concerned Wendy... "Why do ye say that?"

"I was at the gas station Sunday afternoon. The Bernard boy was filling up his car, along with a gallon container. I guess just in case he runs out of gas sometime." Janice leaned forward. "While I was there, another young man pulled up and got out to talk to the Bernard boy. He looked...*shady*."

"Shady?"

"You know. Long hair and sunglasses, even though the sun wasn't out. Wore an expensive leather jacket, too. Looked like a city boy."

"Maybe he was a friend?"

"I don't think so," Janice replied. "He pulled something out of his pocket—looked like an envelope—and handed it over. The Bernard boy gave him some money and then they both got in their cars and left." She tapped her forehead with one finger. "I think it was drugs."

Kevin stared at her. That Dwayne might be involved in something like that had never occurred to him. The drug scene had bypassed Middletown, at least for now. The only thing he'd even heard mentioned was getting illegal beer. But if Janice was right...

Well, he wanted to be a journalist. Maybe he needed to do a little investigating on his own.

Droch sgeul ort! He'd wanted dirt on Dwayne. Maybe this was it.

Maybe the Fae were listening, after all.

****

By the time they got to Government class on Friday afternoon, anti-war violence had erupted again, this time led by Catholic clergy from Cantonsville, Maryland. Two of them had already poured blood on draft cards in an earlier demonstration in Baltimore. This time they set the cards on fire, using napalm.

"Wahoo!" Mark said when Mr. Kyle broke the news that had just come over the radio. "Way to go!"

Wendy frowned at him. "I don't think it's very smart to set a fire in a parking lot."

"Hey, it's called civil disobedience," Mark answered. "Weren't you awake in English class when Mrs. Howell went on and on about Thoreau?"

"This isn't about some guy refusing to pay taxes and spending a night in jail," Wendy retorted.

"And using napalm instead of just a match?" Tim asked. "Do you know what napalm can do?"

"It causes severe burning because it gels and sticks to the skin," Tommy answered before anyone else could.

"Yeah, but people have the right not to take part in something they think is evil." Mark looked triumphant. "It's in Thoreau's essay."

Wendy looked at the ceiling. "Draft cards aren't evil."

"Maybe not, but war is."

Kevin intervened. "Not all war is evil, though."

"I don't agree." Mark stuck to his point. "We

shouldn't have to participate by being drafted if we don't believe in it."

"It's easy for O'Keefe to say, since he doesn't have to worry about getting drafted." Dwayne gave him a smug look. "You're not a citizen."

"We have plenty of troubles like this in Ireland," Bridget said. "Causes that a lot of us believe are worth fighting for."

Kevin nodded. "Bridget's right."

Of course Bridget was right, but did she have to leap to Kevin's defense? And did he have to agree with her so quickly? Wendy grimaced. She didn't have any right to be jealous. Since Kevin had walked away from their group after school on Tuesday, he hadn't lingered after class at all. In fact, he'd hardly spoken, although he had watched Dwayne a lot. She knew they didn't like each other, but she hoped they weren't going to fight. Kevin could get expelled and might not graduate.

"We aren't being called up to fight in a war," Kevin continued, "but the battle against housin' and job discrimination is just as important."

"Oh, right. I forgot," Dwayne replied. "You Catholics get all stoked up about stuff like—"

"This is *not* about religion," Mr. Kyle interrupted. "Some of these activists happen to be priests and monks, or former ones, but they aren't protesting freedom of religion."

"Yeah, cool it about the religious thing, man," Mark said to Dwayne. "We're talking about the *government* dictating to us what we should do."

"Just like teachers do," someone said and several people snickered.

"The U.S. is not a dictatorship, either." Mr. Kyle

gave the smart-mouthed student a stern look. "And neither are teachers, in spite of what you might think." He turned back to the rest of the class. "In fact, teachers have been protesting most of this month in Florida for some of the same reasons we've already talked about."

"That kind of proves my point, doesn't it?" Mark asked. "You guys don't like the rules either."

"It's a somewhat different situation," Mr. Kyle answered, "but your point is taken."

"It just seems like there's trouble and unrest everywhere," Wendy said. "I don't understand what's happening to everything. Why can't everyone just get along?"

"An excellent question and one that is ages old." Mr. Kyle smiled slightly and shook his head. "Regretfully, no one has been able to answer it."

Wendy sighed as the bell rang. How could there be a simple answer to everything that was going on right now? But—and she had been paying attention in English class—Thoreau also said people needed to do what they felt was right.

Maybe one person couldn't make a difference, but that didn't mean they shouldn't try.

****

Kevin was out the door and down the hall by the time the dismissal bell finished ringing. He'd had enough of Dwayne Bernard's derogatory slams. If he had to talk to the guy outside of class, he wasn't sure he'd be able to rein in his own temper.

And Wendy was going to Prom with that...person. What did she see in him?

His mind calmed more as he got farther away from school. Tommy had told him she asked the guy because she felt sorry for him. Tim had said she also didn't want to be Kevin's pity-date. He winced at that thought. He'd never intended her to feel that way, but he could see why she did. And, grudgingly, he could also see where she might think she was protecting herself if she had a date.

A date with someone she felt sorry for.

That didn't make it feel any better.

And if Dwayne was using drugs…

Kevin scowled as he opened the door to Mr. Lambart's office. He'd been racking his brain about how he could prove a drug deal had gone down at the gas station.

Janice looked up as he entered. "You're upset again. Things haven't worked out with you and Wendy yet?"

He shook his head and wondered if she was being optimistic about "yet."

"Well, give it time," she said.

"Do I have time?" Kevin sank into the chair beside her desk.

She smiled benignly. "You young folks tend to be impatient. Some things take longer to work out."

Kevin gave her a direct look. "What if Dwayne tries to slip Wendy somethin' at Prom?"

Janice frowned. "You mean a drug?"

He nodded. "If what ye saw was a drug deal, he could have bought somethin' to slip into her punch or—"

"Goodness! I didn't think about that," she exclaimed. "Maybe I should call Vivian and let her know."

"Wendy would really be mad if ye called her mother," Kevin said. "Besides, Mrs. Wade would probably tell ye to call the police about what ye saw."

"Oh." Janice paused. "I hadn't thought about that either. I don't want to accuse someone of something that might not have happened—even though my gut tells me that's what happened."

He couldn't blame her for not wanting to open up a can of worms that might contain snakes. They had no proof, so he doubted the police would do more than make a note of it somewhere. Maybe.

That meant he needed to get more information, like a good journalist would. "Ye said the other guy didn't stay long?"

"No. Just got out of his car, they said a few words, then exchanged the small package for money."

"Ye're sure ye didn't recognize the guy?"

She shook her head. "I hadn't seen him before."

"Dwayne seemed to be waitin' for him though?"

"I guess." She wrinkled her forehead in thought. "He'd finished filling up the car and was fiddling around washing the windshield."

"That means he was definitely waiting," Kevin said. "That Camaro of his is always shined without a speck of dust anywhere."

Janice looked confused. "Dwayne wasn't driving a Camaro."

"He wasn't?" That was unusual, but maybe he didn't want a drug dealer to see him driving an expensive, slick muscle car. "What was he drivin', then?"

She shrugged. "I'm not good with makes and models, but it was some kind of family car. A dark green sedan."

Kevin straightened. A dark green sedan had been seen speeding away from the Jacksons…

He leaped out of his seat. "I gotta go."

Chapter Twenty

"Dwayne just drove up." Jo peered out of Wendy's bedroom window on Sunday afternoon. "Were you expecting him?"

"No," Wendy said glumly. "I wonder what he wants."

Jo glanced over at her. "He is your date to Prom, and it's next Saturday."

Wendy didn't need to be reminded. She just wanted it *over*. Maybe then Kevin would start speaking to her again. He hadn't shown up for riding practice yesterday. She shouldn't have expected him to, since he practically bolted out the classroom door at the end of each day, but she had still hoped that the horse show would be important enough to bring him over.

"Wendy! You have company!" her mother called.

Jo gave her a sympathetic look. "You'd better go."

"Come with me."

Dwayne was standing in the living room, looking out the window over the yard, when they entered. For a moment, his gaze lingered on Jo and then he turned to Wendy. "Could we speak privately?"

She frowned. "I asked Jo to come down."

He sighed. "You aren't going to make this easy for me, are you?"

Was he going to break off the date? That would be the answer to her prayers! Wendy nearly smiled in anticipation. "Make what easy?"

"I've come to apologize."

Her hopes plummeted like a kite losing its wind. "For what?"

He looked contrite. "I've been kind of a jerk to your friends. Especially to Kevin."

"I guess you should be telling them, not me."

"Oh, I have. Just before lunch." He gave her a tentative smile. "All have forgiven my attitude, except for you."

"I don't have anything to forgive you for."

"That's good, then. I want you to enjoy the Prom."

Somehow, she managed to plaster a smile on her face. "Of course. Thank you for coming over to tell me."

He studied her a moment. "That's not the only reason I came over."

"It isn't?"

"No. When I told the twins I was coming over here to apologize to you, one of them suggested we all have a picnic this afternoon. Their girlfriends have been wanting to see the cave you guys talked about, and I'll admit, I'd like to see it too." He paused. "I don't think Kevin has seen it either, has he?"

"Just from the outside," she answered tentatively.

"Good. Then it'll be a surprise for him and me. Will you go?"

She hesitated, then turned to Jo. "Do you want to go?"

Her cousin shook her head. "I can't. Luke is supposed to be calling me this afternoon."

"Oh. I forgot." Wendy's heart sank. She really didn't want to go anywhere with Dwayne, but if Kevin was going to be at the cave… She didn't want him to think she was the one being snobby if she didn't show up.

"What time did Tim and Tommy say they'd be there?"

Dwayne glanced at his watch. "They said they were going to pick up Susan and Carla right after I left. That should have given them enough time to be there."

And Kevin? Of course, she didn't want to mention Kevin by name to Dwayne. But if Kevin had accepted Dwayne's apology and wanted to see the cave…maybe this would be a good time to try to make amends. She could probably even finagle a way for one of the twins to drop her off at home so it wouldn't look like she was on a date with Dwayne.

"Okay. Let me grab a sweater. The cave's cool inside."

"Sounds good," he said.

As she turned away to get it, she didn't see his diabolical smile.

****

Kevin stepped out of the police station late Sunday morning and put a hand up to shield his eyes from the bright sunshine. Or maybe it only seemed brighter today because of what had just transpired.

The suspect for the two burnt crosses that had been thrown on the Jacksons' lawn was Dwayne Bernard. A warrant would be issued for his arrest.

The detective Kevin had spoken to gave him accolades for what he'd discovered and asked if he'd consider joining the police force. Kevin thought the remark was half in jest since he wasn't a citizen, but he did give himself an invisible wee pat on his back for deciding to do a bit of investigating on his own, like a journalist would.

And thank the saints for gossipy secretaries.

When he'd left the office Friday afternoon, he'd gone straight to the Bernard car dealership, only to find it closed for the day. Frustration had filled him like a cistern overflowing with storm water. If his theory that Dwayne had "borrowed" a car was correct, that dark green sedan would be sitting in the used-car section on the back lot.

Although he'd intended to swallow his pride and go to the horse show practice at Wendy's on Saturday morning, finding out about the car took precedence. Then, to add to his frustration, when he'd gotten there, the doors were still locked. Evidently, in small towns, car dealerships didn't open until after lunch.

Perhaps Janice had been right about young people being impatient. He'd nearly worn holes in his favorite cowboy boots pacing back and forth in his room before heading back out.

And then, he'd had to be careful not to look too eager. He'd picked a fatherly-looking salesman—making sure it wasn't Mr. Bernard himself—and tried to sound convincing that he was saving up enough money to buy a used car for college next year. The man had smiled and obliged—saying he had a son in college too—and taken him to the back lot. Kevin struggled to keep his face impassive.

The dark green sedan was parked there.

****

Armed with that knowledge, Kevin had practically run to the courthouse, where the local city police department had an office. Then he remembered that it was Saturday and "offices" were closed. He'd said a few choice words in Gaelic before finding the gray-haired security guard dozing in the tiny hut that served as a check-in for the parking lot. When Kevin told him he needed to talk to a detective, the man had said he could leave a message. With his string of bad luck, he hadn't put much faith in the message getting through, but he'd left it anyway.

To his surprise, a detective had called this morning. Perhaps the Fae were through with their pranks and decided to cooperate with him.

Kevin took a deep breath as he walked down Main Street toward the car that Mr. Lambart had lent him. Now all that was left to do was drive out to the farm and tell Wendy. He didn't know how she would take it.

"Hey! Kevin!"

He turned to see the twins coming toward him. "Hey."

"We were just going to the Dairy Queen for burgers," Tommy said. "Do you want to join us?"

Kevin looked at his watch. Nearly noon. Wendy's family would be sitting down to dinner just about now and he didn't want them to think he was looking for a free meal. Especially since he didn't know how Wendy was going to react. Better to wait until a little later.

"Sure." He pushed away the thought that he was being a bit cowardly by buying time. It really wasn't good manners to arrive at mealtime. "Where are Susan and Carla?"

"Shopping in Mankato," Tim answered.

"They tried to get us to go," Tommy said, "but we told them we couldn't miss the Minnesota Twins baseball game on TV."

"Whew! Saved by a game!" Tim said as they all

settled in a booth. "You wanna come over and watch with us?"

"I wish I could, but I promised Mr. Lambart I'd detail his car this afternoon." That wasn't exactly a lie. In exchange for lending him the car, Kevin always brought it back washed and waxed.

"Well, okay. If you get finished early, come on over anyway. Mom always makes pizza for us on Sundays."

"Thanks. I'll see how the afternoon goes."

That thought came back to him as he set out an hour later. If Wendy didn't want to talk to him—he'd been avoiding *her* for a while—he would have plenty of time on his hands. He just hoped she'd not blame him for bringing her the news. Shooting the messenger and all that. Although, in this case, he was also not only delivering the message…he was the cause of it. She just had to understand.

Ten minutes later, he pulled onto the yard road and parked in front of the farmhouse. Looking around, he realized he had missed it the past few weeks. The horses stood near the paddock fence watching his arrival, no doubt hopeful he carried carrots or apple slices. Behind them in the field were jumps set up in the same succession as they would be at the horse show in June. He needed to start practicing. With any luck—and he hoped the faeries were still in a good mood—he'd be back on track with Wendy and joining her again.

Jo opened the door when he knocked, looking surprised. Not that he blamed her, since he'd made himself scarce recently. "Sorry I didn't call first. Is Wendy home?"

"No." Jo stepped back to let him inside. "I thought you were all meeting at the cave."

"The cave? By the river? Why would ye think that?"

"Well…" She seemed confused. "Dwayne said you were going to have a picnic."

The hair at the back of Kevin's neck prickled. "Dwayne? He was here?"

Jo nodded. "He said he'd run into you and the twins in town earlier."

"I just left them at the Dairy Queen," Kevin said. "They were goin' to watch the baseball game."

Jo stared at him. "They didn't suggest having a picnic with Susan and Carla?"

Kevin shook his head. "The girls went to Mankato to shop."

"Oh, no!" Jo covered her mouth with one hand. "That means—"

"That Wendy is alone with Dwayne," Kevin finished her sentence grimly. "How long ago did they leave?"

"Maybe forty minutes. I didn't check the clock."

Forty minutes. He'd spent forty minutes having lunch with Tim and Tommy. Forty minutes that may have put Wendy in danger. He'd never forgive himself if…

"Call the police. Dwayne's the guy who threw the burnt crosses, and I think he has drugs." Kevin spun on his heel and flung open the door. "I'm goin' to the cave."

Chapter Twenty-One

Wendy looked around the empty cave. "What time did you say everyone was supposed to be here?"

"Any minute," Dwayne answered. "Why?"

"Well…" She let her voice trail off. It would be rude to say she didn't want to be alone with him. He'd been perfectly nice on the short drive down the road and over the new bridge. "I thought the twins were going to have this all nice and cozy for Susan and Carla."

"It might have been a spur-of-the-moment thought. No problem, though." Dwayne walked over to where a pile of blankets had been folded into plastic bags. He took several out and laid them on the rocky floor. "That should be more comfortable. Why don't you sit?"

Wendy let her gaze wander to two rickety hardback chairs next to a small table with uneven legs. "I think a chair is more comfortable."

He gave her a studied look, then busied himself lighting the oil lamp that hung on a hook above a small brass brazier. "I could light your fire if you want."

Wendy blinked. Did Dwayne just say light your— as in *my*—fire? She must have misunderstood. After all, "Light My Fire" had just been released last year and it was still popular. She probably just switched the words in her head. "It's not cold enough for a fire."

He smiled. "So you're saying you're hot?"

She blinked again. It was typical late May in

Minnesota. Warm if you wore a sweater, but not hot. She shifted her weight on the chair. Had that been some kind of innuendo? "I'm okay."

"You sure? You look a little uptight."

"I'm fine." She hoped the twins would show up soon. "Who's supposed to bring the food?"

"Don't know."

"You don't know?"

"Nope. No one said anything about food."

Wendy felt a chill slide down her spine that had nothing to do with the temperature. "This is supposed to be a picnic, isn't it?"

"Sure." Dwayne reached into his jacket pocket and pulled out a small flask. "I have something to sustain you."

Wendy eyed it. "I don't drink."

"It's rum and coke. Not bitter or anything. Just take a sip." He held it out. "It'll relax you."

"No, thanks."

"Oh, come on." He set the flask on the table. "What are you afraid of?"

You, she wanted to say, then gave herself a little mental shake. She wasn't in any *danger*. She was just letting her imagination run wild since this was the same place Mary Anne had been taken when she was abducted. "I'm not afraid of anything."

He smiled again. "Good. Because I have a little gift for you."

The shiver ran down her back again. "Gift?"

"Uh-huh." He reached into his pocket again and pulled out a small vial which he opened to drop a round, white pill into his palm. "This will make you feel better."

Wendy frowned. "Is it an aspirin?"

"Better than that. It's a Quaalude," Dwayne said. "It'll make you feel all nice and warm inside. I promise."

Wendy felt her eyes widen. "It's an illegal drug, isn't it?"

"Not illegal. Prescription." Dwayne laid it on the table beside the flask. "I saved it just for you."

"I don't need it."

He tilted his head to study her. "I think you do."

Wendy felt goose bumps form on her arms even though she wasn't cold. "What do you mean?"

"I have plans for this afternoon."

"Well, yes. The picnic. What does that have to do—" Wendy stopped suddenly to stare at him. "There isn't going to be any picnic is there?"

"No. Sorry."

She felt her blood start to chill. "Then why did you lie to me?"

"Don't think of it as a *lie*." He slid the pill toward her. "We can have our own kind of picnic."

"I don't want that kind of picnic."

"Come on. I know you really like me. You asked me to Prom. I just thought we'd get to know each other better…" He glanced at the blankets on the floor. "So we'll be a *real* couple."

Suddenly, the blankets on the floor took on a whole new meaning. "I'm not that kind of girl."

"You don't have to be afraid. That's why I brought the 'lude. You'll like what I want to do."

Dear God. What had she done to make Dwayne think she liked him that way?

Wendy swallowed hard. "I don't want to go to bed with you—"

"You will once you take the pill."

"No." She hoped she could make him understand. "We're just friends. Nothing more. I asked you to go to Prom because you always seemed so all alone and I felt sorry for you."

He stilled. "You felt *sorry* for me?"

Wendy winced. Too late, she remembered how much Mary Anne had hated it when Wendy felt sorry for her. She took a deep breath. Better just to tell the truth, then. "Well, not all that sorry. I really wanted to go to the Prom with Kevin—"

"*Kevin*?" Dwayne's eyes narrowed to slits. "You'd sleep with that bastard, wouldn't you?"

Wendy stared at him. Obviously, that had not been the right thing to say either. "Never mind." She rose, forcing herself to walk—instead of run—toward the mouth of the cave. "I'm going home."

She'd only taken two more steps when he was in front of her, blocking the entrance. "You're not going anywhere."

Chapter Twenty-Two

Kevin stepped carefully on to the old bridge, keeping close to the side that still had some of the girders in place. Every slow step felt like it took an hour to his agonized mind, even though following the path through the woods was the shortest route to the cave. Time was of the essence. He'd never forgive himself if Wendy had been hurt while he was blithely eating a hamburger at the Dairy Queen.

Nor had he wanted to take the chance on Dwayne hearing another car approach, unless it was a squad car. One huge benefit of living in a small town where crime was nearly nonexistent—or had been—was that it wouldn't take long for the local cop on duty to get here.

But Kevin wasn't about to wait. He exhaled a relieved breath when he stepped onto solid ground and looked up at the rocky boulders. From this angle, he couldn't see the mouth of the cave, but that meant Dwayne couldn't see him either. Luckily, he was wearing sneakers today instead of his beloved boots, so he had the advantage of silent surprise.

Or he hoped he did.

He started climbing, trying in vain not to think about what Jo had said. Dwayne had set this up. He'd lied to Wendy about having a picnic so he could get her alone. Alone and in an isolated spot. If she screamed, no one would hear…

Kevin paused, the pounding of blood in his ears so loud he wasn't sure he'd hear a scream himself. He took a steadying breath. He had to get a grip. Concentrate. Move carefully. He needed to get close enough that he could hear what was going on. If they were having a regular conversation, he could wait for the police. If they were arguing, he could show up at the entrance and stall for time, saying he'd stopped at the farm and Jo had told him about the party here. Dwayne probably wouldn't believe him, but at least he'd be there to protect Wendy.

And if there was only silence coming from the cave… Kevin didn't want to think about that.

As he got closer, he heard the hum of voices. They weren't loud, so maybe everything was okay so far. He crouched behind bramble growing from a several crevices and crept closer.

"You felt sorry for me?"

"Well, not all that sorry. I really wanted to go to the Prom with Kevin…"

For just a moment, Kevin felt elated. Wendy had wanted to go to the Prom with him! She'd just been mad about the way he'd asked…

"Kevin? You'd sleep with that bastard, wouldn't you?"

Kevin balled his fists. If the police didn't get here soon, he'd beat Dwayne to a pulp for insulting Wendy like that.

"Never mind," he heard her say. "I'm going home."

There was some kind of rustling noise. Kevin crouched lower, not wanting to make his presence known in case Dwayne came out. Once Wendy was safely away from the jerk…

"You're not going anywhere."

It took Kevin's brain a mere split-second to register what that meant. He leapt for the cave's entrance.

****

For a moment, Wendy stared at Dwayne in shock. In the next moment, he lurched forward and sprawled at her feet. It took another moment for her to realize he'd been pushed by brute force, and that brute force was Kevin, now pulling Dwayne up by his collar to punch him squarely in the face. She heard a distinct *crack* and blood spurted from Dwayne's nose.

"You bloody Irish trash!" Dwayne reached in his pocket and brought out a switchblade, snapping it open immediately. "I'll kill you!"

"Leave him alone!" Wendy cried. "Please!"

"Stay out of it, you bitch."

"Don't call her that." Kevin circled around him, keeping an eye on the knife.

He advanced toward Kevin, waving it like a scythe hacking at grain. Kevin dodged and spun, managing to plant a fist in Dwayne's gut. He bent over, but then he charged like a mad bull.

There wasn't much space in the small cave for Kevin to keep dodging. Wendy looked around for a weapon of her own. She had to stop this before that lethal knife slashed Kevin.

Her gaze fell on one of the rickety chairs. Without hesitation, she picked it up, took two steps forward and swung, thankful that she'd played softball for years. Her swing went true, the chair splintering in pieces as it connected with Dwayne's back with a resounding whack.

Dwayne sprawled again, only this time he lay still.

Kevin kicked the knife away just as a police officer

arrived. He took a quick glance around.

"What happened here?"

Wendy's knees began to wobble as Kevin started filling the officer in. She shakily sat down on the one remaining chair.

Kevin gave her a worried look, then turned to the officer. "Can we give you a statement tomorrow? I'd like to get Wendy home."

Apparently, the cop noticed her less-than-energetic condition because he nodded and put his little notepad away.

"That'll be fine," he said. "We've already got cause to arrest him for the racist vandalism."

Kevin nodded and helped Wendy from the chair, putting his arm around her waist to steady her. For a brief moment, she leaned into him and then jumped when Dwayne began to move and groan on the floor. Kevin's hold tightened and he drew her closer.

"Let's go home."

She wasn't going to argue with him. Never, ever again.

****

Wendy turned to Kevin once they were safely over the bridge and across the river from the cave. "Let's not go home just yet. I'll have too much explaining to do."

"But ye're still shakin'. Ye might be in shock."

She shook her head. "I'm shaking right now because we made it over that bridge."

"I'm sorry I didn't bring the car—"

"Don't apologize for rescuing me." Wendy gave him a wobbly smile. "The way you came charging in there…you really were like a knight in shining armor!"

He quirked a corner of his mouth. "I'm nae sure ye

weren't the one doin' the rescuin', my lady."

"I couldn't just stand there and do nothing." Wendy glanced up to where the officer was leading a handcuffed Dwayne down over the boulders. "Come on. Let's get out of here."

"Where are we going?" Kevin asked as Wendy turned into the woods instead of heading for the road.

"There's a little cabin not far," she answered. "I've been meaning to show it to you. Now's as good a time as any."

They walked in silence since the path Wendy took was little more than a deer trail and didn't allow for walking double. A short time later, they passed the row of evergreens that partially hid the cabin from view. Wendy stopped and made a sweeping gesture with her hand.

"What do you think?"

"It looks almost like a classic Irish cottage, except the roof isn't thatch." Kevin tilted his head. "And the walls are stone instead of whitewash wattle, but the settin' with the river so close reminds me of Ireland. Who lived here?"

"I don't know if anyone did." Wendy took the key from its hiding place under a rock and unlocked the door. "It was originally a fisherman's hut, used in the winter when they did ice-fishing. Come on in."

Kevin looked around once they were inside. "This is really nice. A real fireplace and everything."

"Luke helped Jo and me fix it up." Wendy went to the tinderbox and struck a match to light the kindling stuck between logs already laid in the hearth. The fire crackled to life, casting a warm glow around the one room. "Jo and Luke used to come here a lot when they wanted to get away from me."

Kevin smiled as he joined her on the narrow cot. "I cannae imagine anyone wantin' to get away from ye."

Wendy smiled back. "I was probably a royal pest. Anyway, it's a nice place to come if you want to have silence and just think."

Kevin nodded. "I can see that. 'Tis a good place to come to terms with yourself."

"Exactly." Wendy sobered. "I'm going to hate having to face everyone. I was so stupid."

"'Tis nae your fault." Kevin took her hand. "Ye didnae ken what Dwayne intended to do."

"You could have gotten hurt today and it would have been my fault." She squeezed his hand.

"Nae." A corner of his mouth quirked up. "Besides, Dwayne's the one who got hurt, not me."

Wendy closed her eyes and then opened them. "He had a *knife*".

"Aye, I noticed." Kevin's quirk turned into a smile. "The police officer did too, so I'm guessing that will be another charge."

"It had better be." Wendy gave herself a disgusted shake. "I only meant to be nice to Dwayne. I didn't realize he'd get the wrong idea. I really didn't." She frowned. "I shouldn't have asked him to Prom."

"I don't think ye'll have to worry about that now." His smile widened to a grin. "My offer still stands, lass."

Wendy looked at him wide-eyed. "I want that more than anything! I was so dumb to get mad at you in the first place."

"Well, it was explained to me why ye did."

She drew her brows together. "It was? By whom?"

"Bridget." He reached up to place a finger against

her lips when she started to speak. "Bridget told me I was the fool for nae askin' ye sooner. I think she wanted to clobber the side of my head for being so dense nae to realize how insultin' it sounded."

"Bridget said that?" Wendy managed to say.

"Aye." Kevin gave her a tentative look. "Did ye think there was somethin' between Bridget and me?"

"No…well, maybe." Wendy felt her face warm. "Okay. Yes."

"'Tis nothing between us except friendship. Ye ken she pines for Ireland. I think there might be a guy over there that she misses, too." He shook his head. "She looks like my sister Mary, so I guess I took a likin' to her right away."

"I was jealous." Wendy took a deep breath. "Bridget is very pretty."

"Ye are every bit as pretty as Bridget."

Wendy smiled. "You don't have to say that—"

"I mean it." Kevin lifted his hand to push some of her loose hair back and then let his fingers trace her cheek. "Ye are the one I want for my girl."

That light caress sent her brain into dizzying flight. She tried to think, but all that came out was, "You do?"

His thumb slid across her lower lip. "Do ye want me to show you how much?"

She wanted to say *Yes!* but all she could do was nod. Or, at least, she thought she did as she stared at him. Kevin slipped his hand to her nape, cupped her head to draw her closer and then pressed his mouth to hers.

She most definitely must have nodded.

And that was her last thought as her senses took over. His lips were warm and gentle as he slowly brushed them across hers. Soft, but firm, the pressure increasing as he put his free arm around her waist and tugged her against him. Kevin's body was strong and hard as any medieval knight she might have imagined, yet she seemed to mold to him like they were two pieces of a puzzle. Wendy caught the subtle scent of his cologne as she wrapped her arms around his neck, then gasped as she felt the tip of his tongue seeking entrance to her mouth. The gasp was all the invitation he needed and she reveled in the taste of him.

Her first real kiss. From Kevin, who had rescued her as surely as any of King Arthur's knights might have done.

Camelot existed after all.

****

"How do I look?" Wendy asked Jo as she twirled in their bedroom Saturday night. Kevin was going to be here any minute, and she was sure she'd missed something while she was getting ready for the Prom.

Jo rolled her eyes. "I think you've asked me that like a billion times."

"Well, answer it again," Wendy said. "I want this night to be *perfect*."

"Okay. You look fantastic." Jo shook her head. "Although you could probably be wearing one of the chicken-feed sacks and Kevin would think you Gwenivere."

Wendy stopped in mid-swirl. "Not Gwenivere. Kevin's more like Galahad than Lancelot."

Jo looked heavenward once more. "Fine, then. Pick your own medieval princess. You know what I mean."

Wendy grinned. It was true that this past week had passed as if she were in some magical castle in which she and Kevin were the royals.

Kevin had been waiting for her at the police station Monday morning to give their statements to the police. In addition to being charged with burnt crosses and the assault on Kevin with a deadly weapon, it seemed the police had also found a number of illegal drugs when they'd gone to Dwayne's house. His parents had admitted he'd been in trouble before as well as done a stint in drug rehab. It seemed certain Dwayne wouldn't be bothering anyone for a long time.

It had been quite a morning, but when she and Kevin entered the cafeteria at lunch it was to a round of applause. Kevin seemed to take it in stride, but she had turned scarlet before she realized that no one knew about the cabin visit or the kiss. Instead, they were cheering because the news about Dwayne had spread like wildfire after the police officer had been interviewed on TV and had given both Kevin and her accolades about catching the person responsible for the burnt crosses.

Luckily, nothing had been said about her being alone in the cave with Dwayne in the first place. And, to her surprise and relief, the twins had promised not to mention a word of that whole scheme either.

Wendy shook her head, bringing herself out of the memory and back to now.-- she wasn't going to think about any of that anymore. Tonight was the Prom and nothing was going to spoil that.

Car tires crunched on the gravel outside. Jo went to the window.

"Sir Galahad is here."

"Oh!" Wendy pulled on the long white gloves that went past her elbows. "Are you *sure* I look—"

"I'm sure." Jo gave her a little shove. "Go!"

Wendy headed for the door, then turned around. "I'll

see you there."

Jo nodded. "Luke will be here soon."

Wendy paused once more at the top of the steps as she smoothed the satin skirt of her formal. She wasn't sure why she was so nervous. Kevin had already told her he wanted her to be his girl. They'd already shared their first big kiss—and a few others the past week—but tonight was going to be their first real date. She took a deep breath and started down the stairs.

Kevin waited at the bottom and as he glanced up her breath caught. He looked magnificent in a tuxedo, the coat cut perfectly to fit his shoulders. A gold-threaded waistcoat accented the color of his eyes, while the black tie and snowy shirt brought out the burnished copper in his hair which, tonight, he'd tied back in a queue. To Wendy, he looked like he'd stepped from a royal court.

His gaze didn't stray as she joined him. "Ye look like a faerie queen."

Wendy gave him a big smile. Originally, she'd planned to wear one of Mary Anne's dresses, but once she knew she was going to Prom with Kevin, she'd wanted a new gown. The hurried trip to Mankato on Tuesday night had paid off. Her formal was simple—sleeveless with a boat neckline, tucked waist and full skirt—but the satin was iridescent, beginning with ivory-silver at the bodice, gradually turning to pale pink with the skirt transmuting to shimmery salmon with hints of lavender and blue near the hem. The colors seemed to change when she moved, so maybe she did feel a little other-worldly tonight.

Kevin took her hand to fasten the wrist corsage. "These flowers do nae do ye justice."

"They're perfect." And they were. Five tiny white

tea roses, their tips brushed in pink, peach, yellow, blue and lilac. "The colors match my gown."

"Och, well. I asked your mother what ye would be wearin'."

And her mother hadn't said a word to her.

As if on cue, her mother joined them in the foyer, camera in hand. "You can't leave without my taking your picture."

Kevin held out his hand and Wendy stepped into his embrace. His arm wrapped around her waist felt like the most natural thing in the world. She slid her arm around him too, daring a rebuke from her mother by pressing a little closer to lean against his strength.

But her mother just smiled.

And Wendy knew, as Kevin walked her to the car, that this was going to be the most perfect night of her life.

Otherworldly, indeed.

****

The euphoria from Prom carried over into the next week. For Wendy, it had truly been a magical evening. And the perfect ending to it—apart from kissing—was that Kevin told her he'd been accepted into the Global Leadership Adventures program. They'd both be going to the Congo for most of the summer.

The only hurdle left was graduation Friday. The first weekend in June seemed fitting for a new adventure. Just a few more days and they would be high school graduates. Young adults ready to face the challenges of the world.

Or so she thought.

No one was prepared for what happened on the evening of June 5th.

"Stunned" was the word Wendy thought of as students moved from class to class in eerie silence on Thursday. Graduation was only two days away, but it was no longer a priority. Even by the time they got to their Government class, the same question still kept getting asked.

Why? Why had another Kennedy been assassinated?

"I don't know that we'll ever have the answer," Mr. Kyle replied when someone asked the question yet again.

"But the guy was arrested," Tommy said. "Can't they get the answers from him?"

Mr. Kyle shook his head. "All that reporters have so far is that the suspect, Sirhan Sirhan, was a Palestinian with Jordanian citizenship who hated Senator Kennedy because he was pro-Israel."

"But Israel won the Six-Day War last year," Wendy said. "It should be over."

"Just because one side 'won' doesn't mean the other side accepted it," Mr. Kyle answered. "There has been trouble in the Middle East since the time of the Crusades."

"Korea and Vietnam too," Mark added. "We should just keep out noses out of it."

Tim frowned. "Does that mean we should ignore poverty and discrimination too?"

"That's different," Mark said.

"How?" Kevin turned to him. "People in Ireland have been fightin' for her independence for centuries."

Mark shrugged. "But this time it's *our* country."

"Martin Luther King was murdered just two months ago because he believed in fighting against those things," Wendy said.

Kevin nodded. "And that's why the problems in

Ireland and Northern Ireland are heating up."

"And that's the same thing here," Wendy added. "We're fighting a war here. In *our* country. With our own citizens."

"Which proves my point. Don't we have enough problems right here in our own back yard?" Mark asked. "Just look at what's happened to Middletown lately if you don't believe me."

"I'm afraid change is happening everywhere," Mr. Kyle said. "America has been protesting war and rioting over discrimination for the past five years. Small towns can no longer be unaffected."

"Things will never be the same, will they?" someone asked.

Mr. Kyle shook his head again. "I'm afraid not."

Wendy frowned. "It's kind of the end of the road, then, isn't it?"

"Perhaps," Mr. Kyle answered, "but all we can do is go forward."

****

Go forward. Wendy looked at Kevin, standing next to her as they waited in line to receive their diplomas on Friday night. Tonight was the end of childhood. In just a few minutes they'd be presented as the graduating class of 1968…a group of young adults that needed to work to make the world better.

And they *could* make it better. Kevin and she were going to start to make a difference in just a few weeks when they went to Congo. Wendy smiled at him.

He smiled back and took her hand. "A new road awaits us, lass."

One she couldn't wait to travel. With Kevin.

And the *love* beat will go on.

Thank you for purchasing
this publication of The Wild Rose Press, Inc.

For questions or more information
contact us at
info@thewildrosepress.com.

The Wild Rose Press, Inc.
www.thewildrosepress.com